RAYMONDANDHANNAH

STEPHENMARCHE

RAYMONDANDHANNAH

A HARVEST ORIGINAL
HARCOURT, INC.

Orlando
Austin
New York
San Diego
Toronto
London

www.HarcourtBooks.com

First published in Canada by Anchor Canada, a division of
Random House of Canada Limited

Library of Congress Cataloging-in-Publication Data
Marche, Stephen.
Raymond and Hannah/Stephen Marche.—1st U.S.ed.
p.   cm.
"A Harvest original."
ISBN 0-15-603257-0
1. Canadians—Israel—Fiction. 2. Separation (Psychology)—Fiction.
3. Graduate students—Fiction. 4. WASPs (Persons)—Fiction. 5. Toronto
(Ont.)—Fiction. 6. Jewish women—Fiction. 7. Israel—Fiction.   I. Title.
PR9199.4.M345R395   2005
813'.6--dc22   2004017420

Printed in the United States of America
First U.S. edition
K J I H G F E D C B A

To Sarah

I must bring home a man. Sadly, only the bookish will avail to me tonight since there are just academics at Paul's parties, dust to dust to dust. The early fall light is gorgeous over the iris skirt on the bed, and change the sheets, Hannah dearest, just on the off chance.

Hannah thinks about the night

Six days minus Aletheia, and at least five sexless weeks before we finally ended. Why you've been eating so much. All that cheese. All the beef. Fat and greasy and grubby, the stained shirt. Why you've been reading so much. Ha.

Raymond thinks about the night

The sunset has the range of shade that a thick cover of pollution produces as a consolation for city night lacking stars. Violet greens, pink navies, ruddy oranges flood Hannah's attic apartment through a half-dozen skylights. Though Raymond lives in a basement, the weird light manages to startle him, too. August is coming to an end, and so is the evening. There will be parties everywhere tonight where people go to meet strangers who want to meet strangers. There will be a backyard crammed with candles in glass orbs and plenty of booze and a crowd.

The night

If you are male, be five-foot-ten and weigh one hundred and sixty pounds. Be light-haired with blue eyes. Try to have a longish face, and be twenty-five. Your cheeks should be stubbled, and your back should be stooped from carrying bookbags exclusively on your right shoulder. You should also be a candidate for a doctorate in English literature on a seventeenth-century prose writer, preferably Robert Burton. A blue shirt with brown cords is the appropriate dress. In short, be Raymond.

If you are female, be five-foot-six and weigh one hundred and thirty pounds. Have dark eyes to set off your long dark hair. Wear no lipstick. Have two grey hairs already, though you are only twenty-four, and have slightly spaced teeth if at all possible. Wear a tight black shirt and a purple, tasteful skirt. Be smiling. Be Hannah.

Bring wine priced between nine and fourteen dollars.

Shouting over shouting, everyone in the packed kitchen is bubbling up. Young flesh senses the long winter coming. It's as if the party is one big talk, springing from distinct places in gushes of the same laughter.

Hannah is pouring champagne into a clear plastic cup.

"Champagne," Raymond says, "oh dear."

"Want some?"

Raymond rustles through a cabinet and comes up with a coffee mug and a line. "Everything is permitted now the champagne is out."

She pours his Santa Claus mug full of bubbly stuff. "It does make the night more interesting."

Other kitchen conversations

Where to get the best pork dumplings. The merits of echinacea. The poetics of automobile advertising. Che Guevara. The systems of South American ant colonies. Allergies to nickel.

Preliminaries

"What are you here for?" Hannah asks Raymond.

"What am I here for? I was invited."

"You know Paul."

He nods. "And you?"

Hannah sips her champagne. "I'm here to meet men."

A moment's pause, while Raymond casts a critical gaze across the offerings of the room. "What about Jim?"

"Which one's Jim?"

He points to a hippie leaning on the radiator across the room, a large-bearded man in jeans and a checked flannel shirt whose laughter drunkenly booms like dropped timpani over the light chatter. "I realize that I've just ruined it by pointing, but maybe it's all for the best. It wouldn't have worked out with Jim anyway. He's married or something. How about Roger?" He bugs his eyes in the direction of a man in overalls. Hannah looks, arching her elegant neck to see the scruffy poseur affecting boredom beside the refrigerator. "The one in overalls. His name's Roger. Actually I have no idea who he is. I made up the name."

She frowns. "That one's not bad. Excuse me."

3

She reaches for the champagne and refills their cups.

"My name's Raymond," he says.

"Hannah," she replies.

They touch cups, and Raymond again scans the room, apparently displeased with its contents. "The pickings here really are a bit slim. I suggest we inspect the other rooms to see if this is all the night has to offer."

A tour of the house

Raymond and Hannah don't look at other men. It so happens that a series of prints from the Yellow Book is hanging on the walls of Paul's apartment. As they wander, Raymond gives elaborate explanations of the nineteenth-century etchings. The final images are in the bedroom, low above a futon overflowing with coats. The room is almost quiet; they are alone.

Hannah's first impression

At least he doesn't talk about himself all the time, but he does talk a lot, doesn't he?

Raymond's definition by negatives

Not indirect. Not dressed like a whore. Not dressed great. Not desperate. Distinctly not ugly. Not an academic. Not society. Not unintelligent. Not poor. Better not drink too much. Waste not. Want not.

Continuation by way of drawing

"It's very beautiful," Hannah says, stooping to level her eye with the picture of Salome inspecting John the Baptist's head. "But you haven't found me a man to take home."

Raymond, standing, stares down at her crouched

back. "It's so hard to tell at parties like this. One stranger is as strange as the next. But Hannah, let us go back to the party to find you a man."

Hannah sips her drink, and rises. "I do need more champagne."

"What are you writing about?" Hannah asks. They are turned toward each other, leaning on the kitchen table now crammed with empties, full ashtrays and assorted garbage. Paul's family

"Robert Burton. *The Anatomy of Melancholy*."

"You're doing a Ph.D. on melancholy. You're an expert on melancholy."

"I know nothing about melancholy. That's why I study Burton. Can we please stop talking about this? I'm boring myself over here."

"How do you know Paul then?"

"I knew his family back in Halifax."

"When were you in Halifax?"

"Look at him." Paul is slouched drunkenly against a banister on the other side of the apartment. "Looks like a football player, right?" She admits that he does fit the profile: six-four, two-forty, built. "His whole family are aesthetes of the highest order. Frail little English people. His brother, last time I saw him, was wearing a black crushed-velvet suit complete with green carnation."

She is giggling over the rim of her cup. He takes a sip, a small one.

"It's all rebellion. Paul got a football scholarship to university. It crushed his mother. He's the one white sheep in the family."

Her smile opens to a laugh, and she throws her hair back. Her crooked teeth are lovely. "Outside?" he offers.

A private corner They go out for air and find, in a corner of the yard darkened by wind-extinguished candles, two fold-out lawn chairs. Other guests heading in their direction turn aside at the sight of two strangers, probably exchanging secrets in the dark, in the garden.

Luck While he is asking her if she makes it a habit to ask strangers to find her strangers, pigeon shit splatters on the shoulder of his jacket.

"Oh, honey," she says, laughing.

Raymond excuses himself as decorously as a maître-d'. When he returns, he has washed the pigeon shit from his shoulder, and the fold-out chair, the seat beside the woman named Hannah, is still free.

"Isn't there a saying that if a pigeon shits on you it brings good luck?" she asks.

"I've never heard that."

"Well, if it does you must tell me."

He looks up nervously into the branches overhead. "You don't want to move, do you? No, that's too stupid. Like lightning right?"

"You were asking me a question."

"Yes."

"The answer is that yes, I have in fact asked other men to find me men, but neither finder nor found were strangers."

"But that is more in the nature of reconnaissance. Not the same thing."

"It's close enough, Raymond."

"It's not close enough, Hannah. But I have a similar tale." He pauses to fix the telling before he tells.

Secrets about sex. Both Raymond and Hannah recognize that the only way to pick up is to exchange secrets of a sexual nature. What other women do and do not do. Male fears and disgusts. Questions of etiquette: flirtation, penetration, deviation. Betray the past bit by bit. Kiss to tell to kiss. A woman who would never lie down. A man who always, without fail, brought fruit to bed. Strawberries. Pineapples. In a blessed place, it would be enough to describe a memorable orgasm. Instead, in this fallen world, conversation with potential lovers wobbles, searching always for the lower, more dangerous music.

Picking up

Subtle intrusions of gentle wind extinguish the candles one by one. Their endings keep time more accurately than clocks. The dark presses in on Raymond and Hannah's stories, and their stories rise up, one by one, like lighted candles. The sounds of the party inside drift past them and are gone.

In the dark, in the garden

Raymond finds himself saying, "Why am I telling you this? It's the champagne. One-night stands do leave me blank, however."

"Blank?"

Raymond and Hannah find a lower, more dangerous music

"Empty. Never again."

She looks at him sideways. "Is that an unbreakable rule?"

He pauses. "Is that a proposition?"

"Yes."

He pauses again. "Yes." Done. Obliviously and coolly, they head inside for their bags, coats and lame excuses to mutual friends.

Raymond considers the silence

Keep it silent, Raymond, silence along the ride. Your words would fuck it up and reach. Nowtime. Keep your mouth shut. *Fermes ta bouche.*

Conversation in a taxi

"I live in a basement."

"I have an attic."

"Can we go there?"

"I think yes, there."

First journey

The streets proceed tiresomely through the neighbourhoods in which each house tries to be more ordinary than the next. The driver likes dangerous speed but he's still too slow for the passengers in his back seat. They overtake two cars on the bridge. They drive up one-way streets the wrong way. Paid hastily, the driver tears off to race other lovers to other apartments for a little money, and he's gone before the reverberation of the slammed car door. It's a sweet fast song stepping swiftly up Hannah's flights of stairs.

Hannah with her keys

Tarnished burnished metal, bronze silver silver. You've found your keys before. You've done this before, Hannah. The rooms inside are clean and bare. There. That one. Open the door.

To the bedroom, though, ever so slowly they go. **Second journey**
Raymond hesitates to her, and to her bed, where Hannah grabs his neck, pulls him down into her breasts, holds him. She kisses him long, running her hand down his chest, and his fingers fall to her thigh, surprised. Right from the beginning, they must take a rest, going back through extraordinary webs to unbutton their clothes.

When there's nothing left to unbutton but themselves and the other. **Two nudes**

Transport trucks, go slowly. Pull yourself over on **Toronto aubade**
the side of the road. Bring the night with you into your bunks. Let Raymond and Hannah anticipate endlessly on stairs up to attics. Nights in August in Toronto are too short besides. And go slowly, street-washing men. Just let the dirt be dirty for now. Let the streets seize with filth. Let your engines stall, and stop the morning from coming. And more slowly, smokestacks; in fact, completely shut yourselves down. Nights in August in Toronto are too full of light besides. For once let all the power in you not flow, and leave Raymond and Hannah asleep in bed alone.

Here come the Scarborough cars. Here come the **Cities don't listen**
cars from Oakville and the subways full of commuters. In a final thrust after a long blue vein, the

sun arrives, its ore, and it wakes them. It wakes Raymond, anyhow.

The rooms

The woman is curled away from him, and her name, he believes, is Hannah. Raymond extricates himself from the duvet, moving quietly, to ensure she will not wake. At the last moment, he almost reneges. He wants to run a hand through her dark hair. But then there are the unexplored rooms he has quasi-accidentally stumbled into. He takes his clothes into the hallway to change there.

Little to see. There are no books on the bookshelves. There are nails in the walls but they hang no pictures. There are no plants and no chairs and no tables. The only objects that could be called furniture are two green suitcases, one open, the other tucked away in a corner beside a mountain of cardboard boxes. Add to this the light, which is unbearably bright, railing down from multiple skylights at the odd angles of the attic. The apartment is so bare it rattles.

At least there is coffee, in the freezer, beside frozen peas and a bottle of Belvedere vodka. Otherwise, the fridge is empty. There are two coffee cups in the cupboards, then nothing. He checks cupboard after cupboard and they're all cleaned out. Peas, vodka and coffee. This woman knows how to live. She takes it black, one imagines, and he cannot believe just how much fun it is to be meeting women in these cool, brilliant adventures again.

When Hannah emerges scratching her mussed hair, there is a man in the apartment. His name is something. Raymond. He is sitting on a cardboard box, drinking coffee. "You take it black?" he is asking.

A man in the house

They settle themselves in the nook between the wall and the suitcases, the most inviting space on the bare floor. Light from a window at waist height angles onto them hard.

Conversation in a bare room

"I leave the city Saturday." Today is Monday. Tomorrow is Tuesday. Six days yesterday. Call it a week. "I'm going to Jerusalem." This, he had not been expecting.

"Jerusalem. Interesting. Why?"

"I don't know. No, I do know but my reasons aren't very good. I came into a little money, my grandfather died, and I thought, Jerusalem. I'll go to Jerusalem. Until last night, the trip was all I was thinking about. I go in five days. Shit. No, I can't think about it. I'd rather not think about it."

Raymond stares into the hot light that glares from the window, and down to the manicured garden and swimming pool of the house next door.

"And how long are you staying?" he asks.

"Nine months," Hannah replies.

"Nine months."

"There's also the Institute. I'm going to learn Torah at an Orthodox egalitarian institute. The program's nine months long." She drinks her coffee.

"I have no idea what any of those words mean, except for 'nine' and 'months.'"

11

Hannah scratches her hair and shifts herself on the floor. "What it is is a program for North American almost-assimilated Jews like me, who are messed up about their Jewish identity and want to deal with it. And they tell you, this is what being a Jew is, and you are one. Oh, and here's how you do all the things that make you Jewish. And it's in Jerusalem, in Israel."

"I've figured out that you're Jewish now."

"That's a start." When she drinks her coffee, she leaves little dribbles starting from the rim. A lazy lip. The sunlight is powerful and cloying, its force half–sleeping pill, half–aphrodisiac. They let the light drug them while the caffeine kicks in. The neighbourhood where Hannah lives is so wealthy it can afford silence.

"Doing anything today?" Hannah asks.

"Today? I'm going to the university this afternoon, get some stuff ready for the fall. I guess you're not doing anything. No packing or anything. Is your phone still hooked up?"

"No. The phone company fucked up."

"You know, I didn't notice any of this last night. None of these boxes. Didn't see it. You didn't tell me any of this last night. Jerusalem. Bare apartment."

"I had to have my way with you first. Want breakfast?" she asks.

"Peas and vodka? No thanks."

"Dinner tonight?"

He muses, rubbing his hands across his stubbly face. "Happy Gardens? Around eight?"

"You'll have to make reservations."

"I think that's only fair, since you arranged the seduction last night."

"I did not seduce you."

Hannah reaches over and rubs her hand across the back of his neck, as they kiss. Quickly scanning the room while attached to her lips, Raymond checks for his bag, which he cannot remember whether he brought.

Hannah lies down under a direct sun slat on the floor, and throws her hair out, and lets the shadow fall under her shoulder and neck and the small of her back, and lets her eyes go red. Raymond is walking to the university, the clear August day radiating off the windows of every building so brightly, and the ultrablue so heliographical he wants to float into it.

Lightness

Easy. She's going to go no matter what I do and the woman is easy. Dirtiness within cleanliness. Perfect. No mess to speak of.

Raymond considers Hannah's departure

It's summer outside. Inside it is summer. I am the summer.

Hannah considers rightness and wrongness

Men. Other men. With Samuel, everything was all right. Fucking. With J.C., all wrong and I knew it: he didn't brush his teeth; played guitar; wandering eyes and hands. Wrong in just the right way. Mark seemed very right indeed. Violets in hand. Shame-filled eyes. Blood-red ears when it got cold. A blue vein that ran down his face, and a smooth-talking way. That was so wrong. Wrong from the start when you look at it right. Lesley, Mark, Jonathan: right and wrong. That's fair enough. Raymond now. Ray. Raymond. Fuck, what glorious light.

Who gives a shit about books?

Raymond spends the day writing notes toward an insincere screed of his irrelevant opinions on irrelevant subjects for irrelevant readers. Blah. Who gives two shits about the development of copia over the early modern period when you will spend the evening knowing new breasts and how their shapes change in positions of repose? The new textuality of the seventeenth century? Fuck it, something unusual might well be unusually licked in the evening hours. Later is for reading crappy books about the dissemination of knowledge in London, 1485 to 1642. He dreams of the hour he will later snatch for the other one's body, when he will wipe his chalk-dusty hands on the bedclothes. But first, dinner.

Conversation over 3) spring rolls (vegetarian)

The only problem with the restaurant Raymond has chosen is that it has no room for the servers. The square tables (the smallest space on which it is possible to eat a meal) are jammed so tightly together that, to deliver the plates, the waiters have to smile apologetically to the neighbouring tables as they brush them and lean over.

"Tell me everything," Hannah says.

"Everything." He lunges with chopsticks and face both, and slowly chews his half a spring roll. "What do you know about me already?"

"Nothing, and we have no time for evasions like that."

"I need an angle though. That's only fair."

Hannah considers by cocking her head toward the corner of the ceiling. "Professional," she manages to get out between chews.

"Ph.D. student at the University of Toronto."

"Financial."

"Impoverished. Forever."

"Emotional."

"Relatively stable. Unmedicated right at the moment."

"Physical."

"You know that."

"No diseases?"

"None I'm aware of."

"Religious?"

"Not in the faintest. This is fun. I'm being interviewed for a job I already have. Tell me what you think of me." Now she is shaking her head and a hand for a no, and another no.

"We have so little time."

The man at the next table, who ate early and alone, with nothing to do but eavesdrop, grabs his satchel from under his seat and leaves.

"When do you go again?" Raymond asks, after the food arrives. Hannah serves them both from the plates that overlap on the table.

"Saturday," she reminds him.

"So this is what?"

"A fling."

Conversation over 67) lemon chicken and 14) steamed rice

"We established that, I'm sorry, and how do we feel about flings? How do I feel about flings? I like flings."

"You're not alone. They're a hit."

"How do flings work again?"

"You figure it out as you go along."

The waiters fidget in the fragments of space between tables. Raymond and Hannah expect every entrance from the kitchen to be for them, and so a dozen small disappointments sweeten the arrival of the next dishes. Their hunger isn't abated.

Conversation over 23) Chinese broccoli and 83) beef in black bean sauce

Hannah glissandos from the previous conversation, but staccatos the end of the phrase by putting her chopsticks down. "My last boyfriend. Name was Lesley. Ended three months ago. He used to say that the lives between men and women were animal, so there was no point talking it out. But that wasn't it. We needed to talk. With you . . ." she shrugs and picks up the utensils, "we're never going to know. You're not going to know me this week. I'm not going to know you. No one is going to be knowing anybody else, except biblically."

Raymond laughs. "Twenty minutes ago you asked me to list my attributes."

"It won't happen this week is what I'm saying. Once we get over that we're in the playground. Wonderful little fling."

"I'm not complaining. Shut up and eat my food."

"Shut up and enjoy your food."

Though it's almost nine o'clock, the restaurant hasn't slowed in the slightest. Crumbly fortune cookies are delivered with the bill, two minutes after their plates are removed. Hannah skilfully excises her fortune, throws it on the floor, and pops the cookie whole into her mouth. "Don't read it," she says to Raymond as he cracks his open. Crunch, crunch.

Conversation over complimentary fortune cookie

"Why not?" he asks.

"It'll shape the whole night, the whole week."

Raymond reads his anyway. He doesn't bother with the cookie.

"Why did you do that?" she asks, with both real and mock-outrage. Crunch.

"I shouldn't tell you why. You're not going to know me this week except in the biblical sense. Besides, I haven't told you what it said."

He crumples the fortune into a tiny ball and chucks it onto the bill.

"I haven't even asked you about being Jewish yet. Another drink somewhere else maybe?"

Hannah crunches, crunches and swallows. "I think the best plan for this evening is to go straight to bed."

In the initial stages of an affair, it is appropriate to remain within the established realms of foreplay and intercourse. At least within the first month, preferably earlier, fellatio and cunnilingus should be added to the repertoire. While a vast archive of techniques apply to both acts, the use of various modes, steadily increasing rhythms and attention to detail are key.

Carnal etiquette

After the initial stages of an affair, it becomes necessary to widen the range of sexual positions. In these negotiations, assume that shame and sexuality have never been connected, and furthermore that shame does not exist. The options from that point are infinite. Hand moving more slowly than usual, brows arched, eyes looking away, sighs, laughter: these should be read as closely as directives from the judiciary and the instruction sheets obtained with prescriptions.

After a certain, undetermined point, it is fair to vocalize desires, usual or unusual, varying from the back rub to dirty talk to double-fisted anal penetration. The metaphor of food may be useful here. You are not in a restaurant. You are not ordering. Neither are you in someone else's kitchen, where it would be rude to offer advice on the preparation of the meal. You are cooking together, and the mild suggestion is the best plan. Exchange recipes. Ask the other to taste the sauce. Defer to the other's judgment.

If you have only a week, you may compress.

Past cities It's too hot for covers but not too hot for each other, and despite Hannah's prohibition they find themselves talking naked together. The subject is cities.

Raymond worries because, while he doesn't particularly like Toronto, the Nova Scotia town outside Halifax where he was born is loathsome to him. Nothing but small minds and hook rugs. He won't even go back for Easter or Christmas.

Hannah feels proprietary about Toronto, as defensive of her hometown as if it were a kind, drunk uncle. But she's escaping in a week.

They would talk more but they are both asleep.

Morning. Hannah's neck fits in the crevice of his armpit. Families

Hannah wants to know about Raymond's family. Father is an assistant manager at a tourist information centre. Mother stays at home and volunteers. He has two sisters, older by a decade, whom he never sees. No one in his family understands why, with his endurance for education, he isn't running a fish plant or practising law by now. He has learned to accept their confusion, and avoids it as much as possible. Fortunately the folks have recently been distracted by the advent of grandchildren. He is an uncle.

Hannah is an only child. Her parents live in North York and have no clue why anyone would be so insane as to travel to Jerusalem for a week, never mind a year. Currently they're on a month-long cruise in the Caribbean trying to forget how unsafely Hannah is living. The telephone on board is very expensive, thank God.

Noon. Raymond and Hannah have talked themselves awake without coffee. Hannah rises, stretches, and the jingle of an ice cream truck on the street is their alarm.

Raymond's sinewy hips kissing the back of Hannah's thigh. She lowers the boom. That's Tuesday noon. Two o'clock is a spinach and chèvre pizza delivered to a woman in a nightgown in a bare apartment. The afternoon is a labyrinthine flex of joints twisted around each other in a variety of blisses. The red wine Raymond brought spills over the swept floor. Then evening. Raymond's split hand cradles her cunt and she sways it like a fuming censer. The Vs of Hannah's tight hands squeeze against his armpits. Write it all out, Raymond and Hannah, spill it into each other and splash it against the walls of the apartment, the empty apartment with no comfort but flesh. Scream, scream. Scream. That was Tuesday then.

Hannah briefly considers the future

Tel Aviv, Jerusalem, Jerusalem. But I'm here in Toronto, and I will have no Hebrew, no apartment, no grasp. What will I do? How do I make it work? How can I make it work? How do I?

Calm, relax, calm. Lightly, effortlessly, tomorrow and your calm affair with Raymond for the moment. Sleep, sleep. Sleep.

Conversation in the middle of the night

She startles and sits straight up in bed. He had been whispering her name to wake her. "It's nothing. No emergency. I just wanted to tell you that I broke up with a woman named Aletheia a week ago."

"Is that all?"

"Honestly, that's all."

"You could not possibly fuck this up, honey."

"I love it that you call me honey already."

"Sleep."

It's past midnight, dark, and the walls are sweating from the heat at their borders. The fringe of the bedsheet covering the bookshelves trembles in the slight flood of the air conditioning. The skylights reveal the orange urban night. A man's clothes are folded on the floor. A woman's clothes are over them, and the bed sits neatly in the centre, containing Raymond and Hannah who, despite their exhaustion, are talking again.

When she was a little girl, Hannah liked to stay awake into the middle of the night. She would make a tent with the frames of her arms and the covers, and pretend the outside was wilderness, a bamboo jungle she had read about, a desert. Yes, a very bright day in the desert, or the bottom of the sea, the more outlandish the better.

Raymond also had his parallel worlds. In particular, he felt an intense spiritual connection to the woods near his house. He would go into them and collect berries and leaves, sometimes even drying them out to preserve their special powers. Druidic or something. Childhood is its own religion.

Hannah asks if he ever ate the berries, and he did not. He was embarrassed by his own beliefs even then. He was a fat kid. She was skinny.

Which brings up the subject of candy. Hannah recalls that rainbow of sugar you sucked out of a tube. Toffee bricks, Raymond adds, they were a little gross even then. Both agree that the sweetest part of candy was that it was yours and no one else's. Sharing was only marginally better than not having. The introduction to fetishistic materialism happened around age six.

Lost virginities

At sixteen, Hannah meticulously planned out every detail of her encounter with then-boyfriend Rick, including dinner, candles, music and privacy. Hannah willed it. The boy, for his part, was punctual and unfortunate. They broke up right after.

The rejection crushed Hannah, but then years later she saw Rick dancing on a float on gay pride day wearing silver-sequined underwear, and everything was all right.

Raymond was fifteen, and picked up by a girl named Samantha on a visit to Maine for band camp. He has blocked out the rest.

First loves

Each adolescent drama felt as if the earth had fallen out of orbit, Hannah says. Raymond thinks it was more like an airplane going into flat spin.

They must sleep

They must sleep, but already the sky is blushing. This must be what they mean by time standing still: the flow of fluids and information is so rampant, the body doesn't even remember. What day, or possibly night, is this?

Breakfast in the sunroom

The owners of the house, who live on the ground floor, are vacationing and Hannah has keys. They are so rudely hungry from exercise and no time to eat that they dare the downstairs without dressing. Raymond is deposited in the sunroom, while Hannah goes to scavenge in the kitchen.

Moments later, she brings in a vase of sunflowers, which glow yellow on her breasts, bringing her teeth to a sharp brightness and illuminating the underside of her eye sockets. "Wonderful," Raymond says.

"The flowers or the room?"

The sunroom is lined with books and wrought-iron furniture and lovely dank ferns. The sunflowers burnish the low coffee table between them.

"Both. And more."

Hannah smiles and leaves to look for food again, her naked hips swaying delicately. Sitting naked in rich people's sunrooms is a kind of happiness Raymond wishes he had encountered before. Five minutes later Hannah returns with half a loaf of toast and a pot of blackberry jam.

"I have the apartment for practically nothing. The Barths are old friends of an uncle of mine."

"You've done this before. Come down here."

"Yes, they have somebody else to house-sit. We're stealing their bread for this toast. But yes," Hannah says.

"Explain."

"No, it's just that the last time was not under the happiest of conditions."

"Now you must explain."

She simultaneously wolfs down her toast without bothering with jam and reaches across for the pot to spread on her next piece.

"Last time the Barths took a vacation was after a death is all."

"Begin again. Who are the Barths?"

"The Barths are old family friends, friends of my uncle." Hannah curls into her knees. "She wasn't the grandmother exactly. I think she was the mother of his first wife, who died of pancreatic cancer. Maybe her grandmother, and the first wife's mother was dead. A very old person, attached in some vague way, and I mean late nineties, late. She was one of those brittle white ladies, had her share of the regular ailments. I met her just once: totally silent in front of strangers. She died after she decided to stop eating. Who would think it would be so hard to die?"

The sunflowers seem to radiate golden strength like an upturned lamp. Reflections bracket Hannah every time she leans forward.

"Let's talk about something funny," she says.

Raymond sips coffee. "When do you go to Jerusalem again?"

Moving   Somebody has to lug the bookshelves and the boxes down to the Barths' basement. That would be Raymond. Hannah dresses, and leaves the house to bring him back beer as a reward, which they drink in a blanket of skylight. Sweat from the sun mingles with sweat from work and sweat from sex. The only things in the attic are themselves, a bed, and two suitcases.

Hannah on means   He carries shit around. I will carry myself to Jerusalem, fill in the hole of what's missing, interiorily (is that a word?). How will I do it? How exactly? Don't think. Don't. Yet.

At first, it was a considerable advantage in terms of efficiency and convenience that Hannah was shortly to depart. Now, the fact is painful to me. The question is what event separates these two conditions. They are before and after what event? So soon.

Raymond on ends

"I have a cottage," Raymond says.

"I thought you said you were impoverished."

"Looking around here, I think it would be luxurious. Compared to a bare room."

"A day in the country."

"Yes."

"Yes."

"Just like that?"

"Yes."

"Let's go out tonight."

"Yes."

Conversation under blanket of skylight

"Try this," she says, forking over a piece of liver with a bit of onion.

"No," he says.

"You must try it," Hannah insists. "It's the best liver." The pink-grey interior looks slimy, moist.

"You ordered it rare. I don't eat beef rare."

"Try it." Hannah helps herself to a handful of his frites and a scoop of the lemon mayonnaise. He picks the piece of liver up. It quivers gelatinously at the end of the tines. When he can no longer stand the look of it, he pops it in his mouth.

"Terrible," he says between chews. "Truly terrible. It tastes like piss. I don't know how you eat

In the brasserie . .

this." Hannah refills his glass with sloshes of wine and he takes a long gulp, ballooning his mouth, and swallows. "The aftertaste I declare wretched. It must be why you're stealing my food."

"You mind?"

"Of course not."

"At least you won't have to get used to it," she says, reaching over the table to cut herself a piece of his lamb, which she flicks into her mouth, delightedly. "Good lamb," she says, and pauses with her wineglass in mid-air. "I've always wondered . . ."

"What have you always wondered?"

"I've always wondered why men never have clean sheets."

Raymond smiles. "Because then we would have to clean the sheets."

. . . And in the bar . . . They lean against a zinc bar, drinking a bourbon with a twist of orange (him) and a crantini (her). "This feels right," Raymond says.

"Yes it does."

"It feels very right."

"Yes."

"Let's have a second round. I'd like to talk to you more."

"We only have a few more days."

"But that's my point."

Hannah knocks her crantini back. "I want you to kiss my stomach."

They leave his unfinished bourbon with a twist of orange holding down payment of the cheque.

Hannah lies back in his arms in the tub. The water makes Raymond sweat, and makes her need to pee. She lifts herself out of the water and sits down on the toilet. The stream of her piss is the only sound. Raymond is well exercised by the heat. A good soak.

. . . And in the bathroom

"How many times have you been in love?" she asks. Raymond peeks curiously through one eye, because the other is stuck from relaxation.

"Twice."

"How many lovers have you had?"

"Lovers or people I've slept with?"

"Both."

The question requires accurate method: he must first list and then categorize. "Fifteen people I've slept with and two I was in love with, and eight of them, no, nine of them were lovers."

"Including the two people you were in love with?"

"Yes."

She looks displeased, though his semantic precision is beyond reproach. At her somnolent return to the water, the bathtub brims. Raymond lets an arm fall, and water spills over. "Eureka," he shouts, water tumbling to the tiles, and Hannah is laughing again. Raymond kisses her back and they quieten, thinking.

There was Aletheia, then absence, then the party, the morning, the dining. There was the body, the sex hungry, the live ferocity, in the sunroom, in the empty apartment. Then packing and dinner and bathing and passed past passed. Leave it.

Raymond on leaving

This is interesting, because she really is going to go. She has to go. Her going cannot, will not, be prevented. There is no way I will not be left alone. Interesting. Shivering.

Hannah on leaving Forget Raymond and think of the city. Toronto. Home, even with family, friends too, absent. I'll miss it. In the heat, all the air conditioners leak onto the streets, dribble and drabble every few feet. Looks like the buildings are weeping in the heat. For my leaving.

Gratuity Raymond and Hannah take no photographs. In three days, it won't be as though it never happened, but close enough. Species and languages die out every day. The whole world is clamouring with lost things, and every day an army of mourners—editors, lecturers, curators, writers, archivists—rush to preserve the frailest relics of everything we love that vanishes. The vanishing makes us all want to burst into song and to burn something and to blow up. Every library is an incomplete encyclopedia of the vanishing's spread. The stuff we call the material world is leaves that go green to turn red and fall off, and stones ground to smooth pebbles to become dust, and our own bodies and the bodies of those we love.

The bed that night devours them, and they devour each other and vanish. When they wake up, there's rain and it turns serious. One shade lessens and another brightens, as if a sunrise and a sunset are happening at once. Slowly, one kind of laughter dies and another gives birth.

It's raining when they wake up, but mid-morning the rain breaks and they decide to go for a walk. Down to the waterfront, across it and back up; it should be a two-hour jaunt. Somewhere in this city is a lake. If you follow the streets under the shadows of the failing expressway, there is a cheap, plastic zone set aside for tourists on the shore. Children take ferries from it to go to an amusement park. That's where they'll walk.

The waterfront

She has to shout to be heard over the traffic roar as they cross under the overpasses.

In the shadow of the expressway

"I do have a little Hebrew from when I was a kid, from my bat mitzvah. But not much."

"You have a place to stay, and so on."

"No. This is the problem. I mean, I have a room booked in a hostel for when I first arrive, but I'm going to have to find an apartment in the first two weeks."

"Shit."

"Present tense. Let's not talk about it. Let's keep this in the present tense." They've passed under the expressway, the roar of the traffic has fallen like the shadow, and she's still shouting.

"Well, for me, there are two reasons. One is Jerusalem. Israel. To be in a country full of Jews. That's a big thing."

On the beach

"And the other?"

"What I'm sick of is not knowing how to do the stuff, the rituals. I'm happy being the kind of Jew I am. I just wish I knew what to say at synagogue, and what all those minor holidays are. There are millions of them."

She puts her arm through his. "Do you go to synagogue?" he asks.

"Sure. Every once in a while, but synagogue is . . . It's like visiting a hundred grandparents that you never visit. Longing, nostalgia, guilt, warmth, belonging, love. Fucked, all of it. So I'll go to Israel and fix it, yeah right."

Beside the lake, which is so polluted its water qualifies as poison, Raymond and Hannah walk arm in arm in silence. To passing strangers, they could be a nice, young married couple.

At the Harbourfront stage It starts to spit rain. They take refuge under the covered outdoor stage on the water. They sit among empty rows. Their only company is pigeons, but they don't want or need more.

"I've never even been to the Middle East before. I don't know what to expect. It will be one surprise after another."

"That's a kind of expectation."

"And I've read a few books, of course. Guidebooks. Bellow. Friedman." They can hear the rain's volume increase.

"Do you think this should be preserved?" Raymond asks Hannah.

"What?"

"This thing. This fling."

"It's nine months, Raymond."

"There's e-mail. I'm a student. Nine months will pass."

"We have today and tomorrow. Then there's nine months."

"But it's already there. Are we going to walk away from this now? No. We're not. What else are you going to do?" She smiles and looks out at the rain. "Let's just see what happens," he concludes.

"Do you think we can get a cab to drive across the sidewalk to us?" she asks. The rain is pouring now with such violence that they have to shout again to be heard.

"No," he says. "We'll have to wait. Or run."

"Let's run," she says. "I want to get high."

Months earlier, Hannah had received a mysterious package. When she saw the delivery message from the post office taped to her door, she assumed a mistake had been made even before she saw the name over her address: Maximilian Sturplother. It was not the name of the previous occupant, the occupant before that, or anyone related to the Barths downstairs. Hannah even checked the white pages to be sure the name was made up.

Still, the address was hers so she retrieved the package. There was no note, no return address, no identifying information. Inside was a Mason jar full of pot, and not just any pot, but pot so hydroponic and so pure that the buds stared greenly out of a thick coating of THC-crystal white. The angel of marijuana had visited her, and left not even a name to be praised.

Seven joints left The jar fills with rain on Hannah's porch, where it has been cleaned by the rain and emptied dirty by the sun again and again. Inside, they smoke joints one by one, up and up.

Thursday Indoors there are kisses like rain and Raymond runs out to get Portuguese churrasqueira chicken. And all they do, on Thursday afternoon, is smoke pot and eat and screw. Hannah brings fresh rugelach into the bedroom and strips naked and strips him naked in long, unrestrained licks. They fuck in the awkward glare offered by the hardwood floor, while the remnants of meals are spread out in a feast. She sucks his semen onto the sheets. The flesh is all salt: sweat, tears, sperm. Only the cunt has a vague sweet sharpness, like chewing a poplar bud. Every pose must be investigated. Hannah's hair spreads an obscene hand. Raymond's fingers and thumbs become fists.

Sisters His sisters introduced him to drugs. For his high-school graduation, they got together and bought him an ounce. Hannah always wanted sisters.

The rain has stopped, and the only sound now is their talking.

Educations For Hannah, it had always been a question of how quickly she could fulfill the social requirement of having a university education. There were professors she admired and classes she enjoyed, but her ambitions never took shape into a distinct career trajectory at the university. After completing a degree in history and classics, she drifted, worked in a bookstore, as an administrator for a Jewish youth centre, as a sub-editor for a classics journal, all part time. But she hated school, more or less. Most of her close friends left for other cities after graduation. They are mostly out of touch at the moment, lost or away in the various confusions of the end of university and summer vacations and their own affairs. She is alone in the city except for him.

Raymond describes it this way: university was a ship that carried him away from captivity. When it first set off, the ship was freeing him. But he doesn't know where it's taking him, and there's no land in sight.

Raymond has never been inside a synagogue. He Religions has not been inside a church for any reason other than a wedding, funeral or concert. Even while on vacation in Europe, he finds the religious junk stifling and ignorant.

His opinion of Christianity is that it should apologize and then dissolve. He hasn't given much thought to Judaism.

Religion reminds them that Hannah is soon going to Jerusalem, and that everything comes to an end.

The end arriving With the end so close, it may as well be there. Their bodies touching may as well be ghosts in air, so they're laughing.

Also Thursday Raymond collects the garbage in a shopping bag. Hannah washes the sheets to dry them unfurling off the back porch. Then they go out drinking.

A tour of Raymond's library After a little bit more than a little bit too much drinking, Hannah has a truly wild notion: "Let's go to your place tonight."

Raymond sneers at the suggestion. "You must be kidding."

Her playful expression makes it clear she's not.

"My place is not fit for receiving company. The servants haven't buffed the Wedgwood lately."

"I'm starting to think you have something to hide."

Raymond muses with a mouthful of bourbon. "I have a great deal to hide. For example, I'm only seeing you so I can stay in that beautiful attic for a week."

But there's no dissuading her. She must go, and it's about time, too. Why hadn't she thought of this before? Really find out now what kind of man she's dealing with.

She hails a taxi by wading right into traffic. Much laughter in the cab as he warns her that he collects rat skeletons, and that sometimes his homeless friends piss in the sink, and that they should stop off at the Shoppers Drug Mart for calamine lotion because the fleas could leave welts. "One drink," she says, "just a drink."

"All I have is whisky."

"One drink of whisky."

The cab pulls up at the side of a perfectly respectable Victorian two-storey, dark, plain and seemingly uninhabited. Rummaging for his keys, Raymond gives her time to evaluate the unpromising basement door: steel, painted red, set into a cinder-block wall. And inside (lights switched on) is the sad basement apartment, the suicide squat, rooms set off like a rambling romance without the expense of order. Light blue walls, a messy desk, couch and chairs from Ikea. She finds it as depressing as she expected. The shelves are jammed with books: a few scholarly titles and novels, the remnants of an education in the form of beaten Penguins, anthologies of African-American poetry, the odd Aristotle, Derrida, Ovid.

Raymond returns with two whiskys. "Isn't it marvellous?" he says.

"Absolutely wonderful."

"I flew in the best designers. Paris. Milan. Nowhere to find really excellent style on this side of the pond."

"What do you call the look?"

"It's in the impoverished style. Scholar chic." She sits on the couch and he pulls over the chair from his desk. "Oh, but don't sit down just yet," he remembers, "I haven't given you the tour. This is just the library."

He takes her by the hand to the bedroom, where there is a bed and two Paul Klee reproductions on the wall. "Now this room may look like nothing," Raymond says, "but my designers insisted on this one feature." He sits her on the bed, and turns over the duvet. "Feel that."

She flattens her hand against the smooth pink flannel sheet. "They're clean," she says gently, surprised.

"They are."

She smiles at him, and places her drink on the bedside table. "You should be very proud of what you've done with the place."

Raymond looks at his copy of *Anatomy of Melancholy*

Who really gives two shits about Robert Burton? When this is all over, how will you sit at this desk and read this fucking book over and over? Unless women were books, you could do without paper forever.

Hannah considers the goy

When Zadie left all that money for a trip to Israel, he foresaw it. Far-seeing man. All those Jewish guys. A country full. I'll leave the exile behind is the idea, that was his idea. "See the homeland, even Moses did." No more goyish dick like Raymond's here. Nine months of return. Nine fucking months. But Ray's right. It isn't over. Blood is thicker than water. Come is thicker than blood.

They go to sleep in his apartment

Night is more night in a basement. The cats pad through their negotiations at eye level. Underneath pipes slide through the substrata of the foundations. In a basement, dark comes early and light delays. In Raymond's low-ceilinged, dank affair, it feels like you've been inserted into the night as if on a slab. You brush your teeth. You make love. You set your alarm. Perhaps you read before you submit to a period of unconsciousness. The night goes on. The streetcars rumble from station to station. Rats scavenge. Music pumps.

When the sun rises, there will be a day that reaches out, only one.

Raymond and Hannah

The question that comes is how did you fall? Standing at the beam, the gymnast has more than enough ground beneath her feet to balance. Her equilibrium falters, her self wobbles, her poise looses moment by moment. Moment by moment, she falls. The answer is somewhere in the accumulation: the sixth meal, or the eighty-eighth laughter, or the ninth orally induced orgasm. At the fifth, or the eighty-seventh, or the eighth, they could have remained standing. It is the sudden novelty: the way he balloons his mouth with wine; her method of hailing a cab. Otherwise, they could have remained standing. It is the combinations: he stood at the bar with a bourbon in his hand and the smell of frying onion and Charles Mingus in the air. She sat up, stretching from the bed, and there were children outside, gathering at an ice cream truck, at noon. You're not stars in a constellation, not fly and spider, not books in a library (just yet). Now you're lovers.

Falling

First there was peace and quiet. Then love arrived. It ruined everything. For example, all mammals of a certain size died.

The history of love in Toronto

Love came from France and England. It murdered. It lied. It covered blankets with smallpox and sold them. It wasn't needed. It survived.

Love changed slowly, kept coming, straining, rising. It was poor. It was proud. Everybody minded. Love brought with it strange dishes, new hatreds, new forms of exercise. It ruined everything. It survived.

And love keeps pouring into Toronto from everywhere it's despised, ruining everything, with no end in sight.

A day on Enigma Lake

They race to the attic where Hannah's suitcases are. There's no time for the leisurely inspection of the last details, no time for a sad farewell to her Toronto apartment. They have planned it precisely. He will drive her from the cottage to the airport directly. Hannah has her ticket, her passport, and the rest of her portable objects. Raymond has rented a Toyota Tercel. The cottage is near the town of Novar in the Muskokas, on the quiet puddle of Enigma Lake in the wilds north of Toronto.

That is strange country. The highways are lined with factories and mills, and pit stops as large as cathedrals dot the maps you get for free in pit stops. Once you get past the industrial hinterlands, the small towns are poor, the forests glisten with primeval rocks, but the bankers' summer homes are splendiferous and huge, punctuating the wilderness with elaborate wealth.

The cottage is not of that ilk. Having all the amenities, it makes no further pretense. The shelves are lined with odd, scattered books bought, it would seem, by bulk: a few random numbers of the Dragonlance series, *One-Dimensional Man* by Marcuse, *Ghost Towns of Ontario*. The mugs, glasses and cutlery are miscegenated from eight different sets. The tools of cottage life are its furniture and decoration both: paddles and snowshoes on the walls.

At the side of the lake, they calm down from the drive with beer. In the water, great blue herons are snapping at frogs splashing and fish jumping. Canadian nature. The scene is peace, order and good government. Then they look at the papers.

"Holy shit," Hannah says to the headlines. There has been a bombing in Israel. In the photograph, work crews are streaming down Ben Yehuda in a turmoil.

Raymond takes a long slug of beer. "Couldn't you choose somewhere else? I mean, anywhere. How about France? France is lovely."

"Somalia, maybe?"

"Australia?"

"How about Bosnia?"

"They know how to live in Tuscany."

Hannah goes back to the paper. "I'm going to fish," Raymond declares.

"Out in a boat?"

"No, right there off the pier."

She nods and goes back to the paper. Hannah reads the whole thing, every story, every style article including the ones on how to hang pictures over fireplaces and where to buy men's socks. She does the crosswords and the bridge column and the Word Jumble while Raymond casts a line to nothing, nary a nibble. When Hannah has finished the paper, she drifts inside to make a lunch of avocado sandwiches and quartered apples, and drifts a full platter down to the pier.

"This is very Canadian," she says. "Very, very Canadian. It's good for me. You know when I have to be at the airport, right?"

Conversation about fish

"They seeded this lake by accident. Smallmouth bass. Pound for pound the best fighting fish in the world."

"But you have to catch one, right?"

"Yes."

"The hook has to go in the fish's mouth?"

"True. You just finished reading the whole of the Condo Life section, I might add."

"Waste not, want not."

Raymond laughs. "My grandmother used to say that." He pulls in the line and casts it out again.

Interrupted nap

In the afternoon of their last day together, Hannah chooses to nap. The bedroom has green velvet curtains, and when Raymond rushes in he has to tear them back. "Sweetheart, wake up." She startles into the bright light. Raymond is standing there with the fishing pole, a foot-long bass struggling and gasping at its end. "Look at that." He is beaming with twelve-year-old pride. Hannah, groaning, pouts and turns from the light. "Just thought you

40

had to see it," he says, and runs down to the pier to throw it back in the water. Hannah can hear him start to cast again.

That night Raymond barbecues steaks and, because the mosquitoes are thick as smog, they eat inside at the wobbly kitchen table. When she asks him what he thinks about when he fishes, he replies that today he imagined a book in which all the animals of the lake are characters. Fish and insects and the great blue heron all talk with one another. They each have their own world. A book for children. The osprey would be the final chapter. She asks if trees would be allowed to talk and he says no. Why is it that vegetable matter never gets to talk? After a pause to slosh more wine into their coffee mugs, he replies that if talking vegetation were allowed, everything would be babble. Then he savagely chomps a forkful of salad.

Fishworld

"I'm in love with you," he says. "Before we have any more to drink." Hannah takes him swiftly to the bedroom and they become beautiful crisp moaning, whimpering and howling, praising. They turn to a fresh page and return from sex slowly to do the dishes, and return to bed more slowly.

Words mean nothing

At 2:17, Hannah wakes up to Raymond standing at an angle in the door frame. He is drinking whisky and crying. "Come back to bed, honey. I love you," Hannah pleads, and he puts his whisky down on the bedside table and lies down beside her. "You're leaving."

The next morning, they lie in bed, selves enwrapped, examining the bright morning out the window and discussing God.

"It's the minutiae," Raymond says. "Prime numbers. The number of dots on a ladybug's back is always a prime number. I have nothing for that. I have no answer."

"When I think about God, it's strange little moments. I don't know how to describe it."

"Try."

"A dustball moving two inches when a door closes. Things like that. I think, Has that just vanished? I won't remember it. It's oblivion, the story of that dustball. Things that nobody will remember. That nobody needs to."

"Dust moving over a stone seven hundred thousand years ago," Raymond adds.

"Dust moving when you're asleep. I caught a mouse in one of those glue traps once, and I had to drown it, and I saw it there, and I thought, Is that it for this mouse? Is the story of that mouse done?"

Raymond considers Hannah's mouse. "Okay. That one's weird."

"I go to Jerusalem today."

"Holy shit, you do."

Hannah swims out into the Canadian lake and Raymond returns to fishing, eventually catching his old friend the big bass again. She treads water to watch his delight. "You've already caught that one," she says.

"I could catch this fish every day of our lives," Raymond says, letting it slither out of his hands into the dark under of the lake water. "Come out of the fishworld, Hannah. Let's take you to Jerusalem."

Overpasses are built for confused anticipation. Highways are built for silence. Lovers are built for crying, Hannah for leaving, Raymond for staying. Airports have clean lines. Their arcs are exactly geometrical, in white and matte chrome, pink and grey plastics, rubber and steel. Airports are built for Raymond waiting at doors that slide open and shut, and Hannah running through check-in, through security, through the tunnel to the airplane to sit and consider what that was.

Architecture

Let me get it together. Hard material considerations. Let me say what I know. Raymond will walk beside Lake Ontario. I will stir my finger in the Mediterranean. We are flying close to the sun.

Hannah in flight

No. I met a man named Raymond, who was exactly what I wanted. Lighthearted, hungry for the world, worldly hungered, like a city running with ravines. Blue-eyed Raymond, man-smelling, kind. I departed.

Let me say what I know: what was that? We might be drinking sweet drinks in dark bars and take a cab through the streets, out through the parks, down to the lakeshore. He made me laugh, made me glisten with sweat, and listened. Our glasses were always filled with wine. Never bedroom shy, he taught himself my cavities, cold-hearted coitus, spilling me on the sheets.

Now I head through the sky to Jerusalem, close to the sun. Thirty thousand feet, the air is frozen. Yes. Earthy Raymond grounded and I'm hung in the middle of the sky.

Next nine months Date: August 31 (4:14:27 pm)
Subject: Next nine months

Dear Hannah,
Right now you're somewhere in the lithosphere, I think, looking down on the coast of France, and I'm full of fragments of meals, sex, talk. Meeting you over champagne. The bath. A piece of liver. Rain on the lakeshore. That drawing of Salome. It seems like we did nothing but eat and screw. The bed was an island, and we made sorties for food. Now we go to the opposite extreme, I guess.
I love you.
Raymond

Raymond considers women in time Friend (who was it? what was his name?) used to classify all women by the time he thought he could spend with them. One-night women. Six-week women. Other women were good for a year. A lifetime, some. And what kind of mixed blessing is it that when I really feel like communicating (struggled with that word), I can write to an infinitely complex series of wires spinning entirely to themselves?

Date: August 31 (4:22:15 pm)
Subject: Me again

Hannah, that was fantastic. What was that?

The sun should not be shining in that place, but there it shines. There it remains as the passengers put their tray tables up, raise their chair backs upright and turn off all electrical devices. Below, the Mediterranean is a broken white grid of waves on the water slowly rising to meet them.

In the seat behind her, a Central European accent is offering advice to his neighbour. "All of these things you will see in Israel, you see them in two minutes." The tourist's voice is an indecipherable murmur, and Hannah can't make out his words, but the other man, the one with the accent, comes through clearly. "I mean this: I mean that you can never be more in Israel than when the wheels of the airplane first touch the tarmac. That is Israel. And I mean the rest is built around it. It is like a very nice refugee camp built around an airport. A refugee camp in the mode of a country." The tourist makes questioning noises. "By war" is the answer.

The Mediterranean Sea, the ancient sea, and what she sees is the pattern of waves on the shore of Enigma Lake, a gasping fish at the end of his line. She hears his voice.

I'm landing in an entire fucking country of nothing but Jews, and why am I hearing him?

Jesus died here. Mohammed leapt into the sky.

And now we're landing. And I'm hearing the landing: rubbersqueal, machinemeal, tempered wheels and flows the hard rush of the thrownback flaps. The airplane slows down to silence before everyone stands while they tell us to sit. And I'm here. Where I planned.

Hannah arrives in Jerusalem

As soon as Hannah deboards, despite her better judgment, she buys a pack of cigarettes and smokes two with an instant coffee at a café just outside the airport. Here and now is a desert, and therefore it is hot. Here and now is Israel and therefore the people are Jews. The brand name of the cigarettes is Time. They smoke Time here. She must absorb the facts through the fogs of travel and alteration and tobacco. She should figure out how much money she should change and find the paper scrap with the name and number of her destination written on it. In a taxi shared with two businessmen, she crosses the width of the country in what seems like ten minutes. No time to adjust to the shape of letters on the billboards or the weaponry in the soldiers' hands. Impossibly white, Jerusalem rises out of the black hills. The businessman beside her smiles. "Très blanche," he says to no one in particular, "Jerusalem est magnifique la première fois." Magnificently ordinary to Hannah, the city of God is full of ugly highways, and traffic lights, and apartment buildings wrapped in lines of dry-ing laundry. The cab drops the businessmen on quiet residential streets, which are frankly suburban (does God watch over suburbs?), then plunges downtown toward Jaffa Gate for Hannah. She is alone, in Jerusalem, and ragged to the bone. There are only two things that make sense: more coffee (again instant and disgusting) and more cigarettes. The space in front of David's Tower is filled with tourists and what locals think to sell them: kipahs, carved wood animal figurines, film and ice cream. Her hostel is somewhere in the covered maze beyond their stalls. Already she has memories of Israel: she has seen every kind of Jew there has ever been. Red-haired Davids with their Solomon sons. Abrahams with their Isaacs. Rabbinical students of the mystic Nachman of Breslov. Zionist cowboys and teenage soldier women. Survivors with numbered wrists. Dandies from St. Petersburg in elaborate outfits. Bankers from London and Paris. Warriors out of Gilead. Socialist dentists from Detroit. Orthodox rabbis' wives with rabbi sons. After the coffee, she can see better. There is a store where she can rent an Internet connection for twenty minutes.

Date: September 1 (10:11:55 am)
Subject: Having just arrived

Dear Raymond,
Hello. I am jittery. I cannot seem to keep an organized account of my thoughts, my plans and my resources.

In less than two weeks, I have to register at the Institute, find an apartment, and deal with all the other shit like bank accounts, phone lines and Internet connections. I put all of this out of my mind in the delirium of last week, and now I'm going to go bananas.

It did me some good to read your e-mails. I meant what I said.

I guess we know what we're doing.

Even if I don't.

Love,

Hannah

Sleep A room in a hostel, however squalid and small, is private enough for crying, thank God. Crying develops into sleeping. Sleeping takes ten hours.

It's so dark when she rises, and she's so in Jerusalem, in the Old City, and she's so alone. There are pigeons on the cobblestones in front of the hostel.

Pigeons in Jerusalem The pigeons fly into Jerusalem from Hebron, from Beirut, from the Golan, from Gaza, from Tel Aviv, from Cairo. They can't tell the difference. They do not even have the intelligence to revere the holy places and the fences between them. They flutter each other in front of the Dome of the Rock, and unsteadily drift down the next moment to hunt crumbs beside the Wall. They cross east to west, west to east; their judgment is indifferent: they shit on the heads of Jews, Muslims and Christians, Greeks, Arabs and Armenians. At the sound of the first bursts of gunfire that spreads onto praying backs, or weakly thrown stones, or nail bombs shrapnelling children's faces, they scatter.

In the stalls, she searches for a good map so she can find her way to the apartment listing board she was told about months before. When? Where? What? Dust, covered women, machine guns, running water, leering men, cut melons, cigarettes, underwear, ground coffee, the shifting eyes of a hologram Jesus. The stones themselves seem to call out for her money.

Hannah in the city

Date: September 4 (6:43:42 pm)
Subject: Arrangements

Arrangements

Dear Hannah,
The papers are full of Israel again. The photograph of a bomb scene showed various Orthodox forensic teams running through the site collecting body parts. The reporter explained that they need to have everybody's body in the right place for burial, because of some Jewish resurrection principle.

I think about your body. My travelnik, I'm sure you're still in the fog of travel, but tell me you're okay.
Love,
Ray

Date: September 7 (2:33:51 pm)
Subject: re: Arrangements

Dear Ray,
I strongly suggest that you learn to stop worrying after each bombing, because you will have nine months of perpetual worry otherwise. Besides, that was Tel Aviv and I'm in Jerusalem.

Now I'm going to clarify myself to you.

My brain is double-fried from trying to normalize myself to an abnormal place and recover from our week. Now I'm fucking missing you. There is also the fact that my life has been consumed with survival details and other little things like that. It is exhausting and frustrating and no way to enjoy a country. Fortunately, there are Internet cafes on either side of my hostel. Both seem to be run by Russians and inhabited by Americans. Here is another unhappy feature of the landscape: I am surrounded by students again. I have been staying at the Israel Hostel (imaginative name, no?) and have been trying to reduce jet lag, but members of a youth group from Cleveland keep showing up in the middle of the night drunk out of their minds. And I need sleep: searching for an apartment in a city where you don't speak the language is hell. I have been to the Wall once (it is a wall), and the other tourist spots will have to wait. I am simply too tired.

Last night was filled with explosions powerful enough to wake me, and when I asked at the desk what the gunfire was about, the man barely looked up from his magazine. Firecrackers. What kind of lunatic wartorn country is this where they celebrate with fucking firecrackers? Already I am no longer fazed by the sight of eighteen-year-old girls brandishing Uzis at the local corner. There are guns everywhere. I think, with hindsight, it wasn't so smart to pick a hostel in the Old City. The tensions are naked even though Oslo is on track and there hasn't been too much violence lately, at least in comparison.

Oh, and everyone here is rude. They treat you like family, that frank and that presumptuous, which is less charming than it sounds.

I'm going to try and survive for a while.
I miss you ludicrously.
H.

Date: September 9 (11:23:43 am)
Subject: re: re: Arrangements

Dear H,
I read somewhere that culture shock's more severe coming home than going away. Can this be true? Are you very homesick, desperate, lonely?
Hoping not,
Ray

Date: September 11 (7:22:17 pm)
Subject: re: re: re: Arrangements

No, no, no. Even with all these troubles, Jerusalem est magnifique. It is like walking through a physical allegory, at least in the Old City. It's like living in an allegory where they want to sell you tchotchkes all day.

You must not worry about me. I look at all these American undergrads and I figure I must be able to find a way. We will be in touch (how sad that the expression is just a figure of speech). Maybe you should come and visit me. Soon, please God, I will have an apartment, and you will "know someone in Jerusalem."

I must go get a little sleep before it's broken by goddamn firecrackers and goddamn students again. They haven't yet moved on.

Tell me the details of your life.

I love you,

H.

How to look at an apartment in Jerusalem

On the phone, make confused agreements in multiple pidgin languages as to date, time and location for an apartment viewing. Hide your cigarettes. Mint your breath. Show up early and wait. Continue waiting. The middle-aged man or woman will arrive already irritated that you insist on inspecting the place before renting it.

Observe the linoleum, the proximity of the highway, the unconditioned heat. If you want the place, which is unlikely, it is taken and also too expensive. If you don't want it, it is cheap and in a good neighbourhood.

Bring American cash. Forget it at home when you need it.

Date: September 13 (8:37:00 am)
Subject: re: re: re: re: Arrangements

Further arrangements

Dear H,
In the clear light of day, I can see that you're right. About the bombing info situation. An arrangement will have to be made, even if it's just with myself.

We have now passed almost twice as much time apart as together, so if we were a cocktail, we would be two parts absence, one part presence.
Love you,
Ray

Date: September 14 (9:12:03 pm)
Subject: re: re: re: re: re: Arrangements

Dearest Ray,
But I asked you for the details of your life and you must satisfy me, because I need escape right now. Tell me something really boring about Toronto. I'm already fucking sick of being in Jerusalem.
Love,
H.

Saturday, September 14, is the Jewish New Year, and Hannah has nowhere to celebrate, no idea

Rosh Hashanah

where to go. In Toronto, she could have found a half-dozen services within walking distance, but not in Jerusalem.

Wondering why she travelled so far to be more alienated from her people, she spends the holiday mostly sleeping and strolling, and in the evening, after she has finished her message to Raymond, she realizes that she didn't even try to hear the shofar blown.

Jerusalem is a room

Hannah, stepping out of her hostel door into the shadows of the covered city, could have God or violence or both, but what she wants is a room that is hers and nobody else's. She longs for her bare apartment with Raymond in it. By the beginning of her second week of apartment hunting, Hannah has officially resumed smoking. Smoking is the same in every city. You light a match, and you inhale. The city is at its most naked: rooms to live in, means to get to them, garbage on the streets between.

Hannah considers garbage on the streets of Jerusalem

Pizza boxes, pop cans, newspapers, styrofoam, mangled in every corner. Jerusalem is never cleaned, it appears. Like the stones placed by visitors on the graves on the Mount of Olives. Waste clogs the corners, and what corners. Recognition clogs the streets.

Homesick

These people are not my people though they are my people, and when I reach I cannot ever know what I will touch. That's the thing. To be pacing comfortably, with no bag over my shoulder and fancy shoes on my feet, across College Street, Bloor or even Yonge Street, or . . .

No apartment, cigarette and coffee, cigarette and no leads, cigarette, where are my quarters, James? Well, I've started again, program begins in four days, fuck, and another coffee.

Desperate

And no man to bring home. Raymond, Raymond the clean-sheeted. Or under the skylights in the apartment. To walk down Avenue Road with him. Not for nine whole months.

Lonely

Date: September 16 (8:37:56 am)
Subject: Things will work out

Things will work out

Dear Hannah,
You will not be so tired and alone when you find an apartment and that will happen. At the last minute, it always does.

You ask for escape in the details of my life, and so here they are. I walk to the university in the morning and fool around in the library and then I walk home. There are occasional digressions for bookstores or parties but they are rare. Sometimes, I go for a walk along College Street for a change.

"Seek for food and clothing, and the Kingdom of God will be added unto you." That's Hegel, I think.
Love you,
Raymond

Then the first day of Hannah's program arrives, right on time, too soon.

The Institute is located on a wide street far in the city's south, a street of dealerships and discount outlets mostly. Mercedes-Benz has a huge warehouse on the corner, and there's a bulk grocery club and smaller strip mall storefronts selling mattresses, cellphones and guns. Every pedestrian under the age of thirty heads toward one particular door, so Hannah knows it's the one. There's also a small bronze sign over the lintel to distinguish it from the other outlets.

It sells a product too: the atmosphere of authentic but non-threatening Judaism. In the reassuringly ordinary foyer, two hundred people or so are milling about, searching for avenues of introduction and conversation. It reminds Hannah of summer camp, the only other time she has been surrounded entirely by enthusiastic, engaged young Jews who make her feel awkward. She will have to buy new clothes. Jeans and a T-shirt are not so inappropriate that people stare, but almost every woman in the building has discreetly, without overemphasis, covered herself from ankle to wrist. Some of the female teachers (they must be teachers, the older women) even wear the shapeless orthodox hair coverings. Hannah finds her name tag on the table just as an intercom voice announces that orientation is commencing in the lecture hall.

"Shalom," says the young rabbi, who has been waiting at the lectern for the hall to fill and settle.

"Welcome to the beit midrash. My name's Menachem. Just Menachem. Don't bother with Rabbi. Don't bother with Doctor." The Cool Contemporary Rabbi Who Knows What Young People Are About. Hannah has hated every example of the type she has ever met.

Menachem explains the order of learning for the year, and outlines the guest lecturers slated to appear: mostly professors and rabbis, with a scattering of eminent and semi-eminent men of letters. In the early morning, there will be biblical Hebrew classes for those who need them, and in the afternoon havruta learning. The repetition of the information is reassuring. She is at least in the right building. Menachem drones on about principles of study and the traditions of the magnificent rabbis and their confusing, boring disciples. Hannah's confused and bored already, exactly like drifting off in synagogue on the other side of the Atlantic. At least there's air conditioning. What was that word? Havarti? *Omertà*? What?

"If you don't know what a havruta is, don't sweat it, we're going to get everybody a partner after lunch and do a little practice. And if anyone is looking for an apartment, come and see me now. We have a few vacancies and connections. Okay, you're free. Rabbi Katz will be giving you an introduction next week. There's brunch outside."

An Israeli would be out of place here, in the English-speaking, synagogue basement–style

Hannah isn't bored when the rabbi says . . .

Americans

rooms filled with United States citizens, their talk, their food. Ivy League, Jewish-American youth has found a pocket in the City of God, and set up a brunch with bagels and lox, and drip coffee from a percolator, which Hannah has been craving since the day of her arrival. She sees two women dressed, like her, in T-shirts and jeans, and she's drawn to them instead. They have their names pinned to their shirts: Deborah and Jenn.

First impression of Deborah

This woman will know what a havruta is, and even for a stranger, such soft, grey eyes, low brown skin, ingenuous lips.

First impression of Jenn

Smiling nervousness, apple-cheeked urbanness, secretive openness. Hard to pin down.

Meetings after brunch

Hannah introduces herself by remarking on the similarity of their outfits. "I feel naked in this," Deborah says. "Imagine feeling naked in a T-shirt and jeans. I thought it was fail-safe. I mean, it's the desert out there. Don't even get me started."

"I know what you mean," Hannah replies, "I'm going to need a new wardrobe." Her first snatch of talk without a business motive in weeks, this morsel of conversation is strange and familiar, like putting on old clothes, but it does feel good to be around people who aren't sellers, servers or landlords.

"You're the one still looking for a place?"

"Desperately," Hannah says.

"I know we have one room left to fill. It's the smallest room, and the rent isn't very cheap, but it's in a good neighbourhood. The German Colony."

"Can I drop by tonight?" Hannah asks, betraying overmuch her urgency, a social novice again.

"Come right after havruta. Everyone will be there then."

"That's another thing. Do you know what a havruta is?" Hannah asks.

Jenn interrupts. "Have either of you got partners yet?"

"Marcia's my partner," says Deborah.

"You're my partner then, Hannah. No choice. I guess it's true what they say, that once you leave school you get a job with people who dress like you." Meanwhile the others are filing into a large room to the side of the lecture hall.

The room is large and divided by two long tables, set with facing bookstands at which two partners, or havrutas, will sit. There they will debate the chosen texts across from each other, like a game at camp, except that it takes a lifetime, or in this case a year, to play. Hannah had better get used to her partner's face. A tall woman with a long back, curly blond hair, unreconstructed teeth and shining hazel eyes. Jenn. For this practice session, Menachem gives them a single line from Genesis to study.

"'And God saw that it was good.' That's the line," Hannah says.

"The whole afternoon on that one line. More than enough, right? Do you want to go down the

"And God saw that it was good"

59

paradox road or what? Whatever's fine," Jenn responds.

Hannah hesitates, but thinks she understands. "That God is all-seeing so why does He see?"

"Yeah. Why does He need confirmation that it's good."

"No. How about why does God choose to see?"

"You mean why doesn't He just look away?"

"Yes." Hannah's partner looks at the line again.

"The key is it's not mechanical. Like, it's not a clock ticking away. He makes it, yes, but He looks at it too."

Hannah needs to fill in here. "Right. It's not like the Greeks. It's not Greek. In the Greeks, the gods don't really see. They're too busy out having sex. I guess sometimes they see, but it depends on where they are. They have perspective. God has total vision. He is being, but He is also seeing." Jenn is looking intently at the line again. "But maybe I'm going down the paradox road. Which we don't want to go down."

"No. I think you're right. I think He is a Jewish God. He's nosy, that's how you tell. You know, if He'd looked away, everything would have been fine. He's watching when you don't want Him to watch and He's not watching when you want Him to. This whole book is His bloody looking problem. And He won't shut up either. You know, I have my suspicions about this line. When's the next time He sees something good? Never. It's like my aunt; hates all the men my cousins bring home, but she always likes the first one. So she can say, 'I don't hate all your boyfriends. I liked Tim, or whoever.' Same thing here. If somebody tells Him, 'Hashem, blessed be Your Holy Name, you hate everything,' He can say, 'No I don't Remember the darkness and the light?'"

Hannah thinks, This is a real Jew, the New York kind. Not a princess. Fun.

Leave school with chatty Deborah, discussing various facts and rumours about the Institute head, Rabbi Jack Katz. Walk down from the school through the German Colony to a three-storey house built in white Jerusalem stone.

How to find your apartment

Inside, smell the vegetable greens and soy sauce, hear the distant crinkle of kitchen laughter. Shake hands with your future roommates, who are named Pamela and Jodi. Both are plain and from Delaware, but still, this is your apartment. Even from the front door, seeing the clean tile floor, the well-kept drapes in orange and purple, the wall hooks with dangling key chains, you know.

The smallest room will be yours. French doors connect it to Deborah's room, but she has covered the glass with a thick Peruvian blanket. There are dust flurries and hairballs from a previous tenant in the corner. There is a single bed, a shallow desk, two chairs, shelves. The window looks out onto backyards through the branches of a pomegranate tree. Beautiful: a place to think, study, learn.

Take it immediately. Deborah will smile. Call a cab for the Israel Hostel to pick up your suitcase.

Date: September 20 (2:04:14 pm)
Subject: Your last message

Hannah,
For some reason your last message didn't get through entirely. Cut off at the word "identity" for a cosmic, technical joke. We can forgive the geeks that, among the superabundance of messages banging around outer space, one will be lost from time to time. Could you resend it?
Love,
Ray

Date: September 22 (9:02:02 pm)
Subject: Settlements

Dear Ray,
I did not save my message. I will do so in the future.

But that's okay. My only real news is that I am finally settled, or as settled as can be. I have a wonderful apartment with wonderful people from the Institute. It worked out at the last minute just like you said, thanks God.

Our place is in the German Colony, which is an increasingly hip part of town. (I didn't believe there could be a hip part of Jerusalem, but there are the pseudo-hippies, pseudo-entrepreneurs, pseudo-literati just as in any other city.) My room has the barest of glass doors to divide it from Deborah's room, but we are both single and easy to live with. There's one of those weird

South American wall hangings across the glass. I'm not going to ask. Deborah is becoming a good friend.

I'm also falling in love with a woman named Jenn who does not live with us but studies with me most afternoons. Jenn's husband is a guy named Niklas who's a doctoral student from Finland. He is doing his Ph.D. on alcoholism in Finland, or something. Jenn is hugely smart and tough, just the kind of woman I love. Her life story is stranger than fiction: New York, Finland, Judaism, Jerusalem. Suffice it to say, I am glad somebody else is with a goy. That's like sacrilege here. Very bad.

By my standards, the apartment is a very Jewish place. The house is kosher, which I can deal with, but Shomer Shabbat is tough. Nobody can turn on any lights in the house on Friday night or on Saturday until after dinner. No one can rip toilet paper or cook. I have never seen that, never mind done it. Or not done it.

The authentic Jewish experience is not all latkes and spice boxes.
Love,
H.

Date: September 23 (10:04:54 am)
Subject: re: Settlements

Dear Hannah,
I'm sacrilege where you live, that's fascinating, but we must never discount the erotics of the

taboo. Tell me more. That could not have been your whole message.
Love,
Raymond

On the day of atonement, Hannah is so busy setting up her room, pushing furniture and laying down rugs that she has forgotten to have a big meal before the fast. There had been fair warning, too: in the souk, two days earlier, she had seen the Orthodox men praying with chickens, which they later kill to expiate their sins.

At three in the afternoon, at the peak of the fast, she breaks down and rushes to Arab Jerusalem where she consumes a falafel, three coffees and five cigarettes, roughly in that order. Walking home through crowds of pedestrians, she notices businessmen in suits wearing running shoes. Then she remembers why: the prohibition against wearing leather on Yom Kippur. But a few men are dressed all in white, which she has never seen before and doesn't understand. She'll learn about it sometime soon, she figures.

The windows were open, snatches of family songs seeped out, the smell of well-loved dishes, the rattle of plates, when I walked through Jerusalem last Saturday. You need a family in Jerusalem. Toronto is a good city to have no relations, a good city for a brief affair. Pick up at a party, fall into bed, consume a plate of liver, splash into Canadian water, and leave it at the end. A good city for Raymond, and I love it. But closed windows and dirty laundry and snow.

There is a knock on the door while she is prepping for her biblical Hebrew class. It's Deborah. They will all be eating Shabbat dinner together; everyone under the roof on Friday nights will be seated at the dining room table. Pamela and Jodi smile warmly at their new dinner partner, and a hot plate on a side table dispays their labours: a chicken in lemon sauce, kasha, broccoli and an apple crumble.

Three men have come for dinner, Moishe, Judah and Rick, three wise men bringing wine, challah and gratitude for the invitation. All three are wearing yarmulkes, even balding Judah.

For Hannah, the rest of the evening is a blur of misunderstandings. The sung prayers, the breaking of the bread, the drinking of the wine are all elaborate rituals, and seem to go on too long. Then there's the handwashing, which she has only done at Passover before. She mouths the traditional Hebrew songs, because she has never heard them and doesn't know the words. Her own family said "good Sabbath," lit candles and that was that.

There is a great deal of talk about each person's journey into Judaism, into living Jewishly, and then Rick gives a small informal sermon, whose conclusion is that Judaism is now and always has been ecologically friendly. Later, Deborah will explain to her that Rick is giving a Dvar Torah (a word on the Torah) about the week's parsha (Bible portion). Hannah has only vaguely heard about the practice.

Conversation turns to the subject of the rosh yeshiva (head of the Institute), Rabbi Jack Katz, about his learning, which is enormous, and his past, in which he was a Christian once, in the sixties.

Hannah notices that, all through the discussion of the rabbi, Judah is pursing his lips and offers none of his own opinions on the man. Deborah later explains that there is a prohibition against loshen hora (gossip), and that Judah disapproves. Learning that gossip is forbidden, Hannah takes a long drink. The sweet wine must be kosher.

Hannah tastes kosher wine

Burning saccharine grapejuiceness, better swallowed than tasted. With Raymond, it was cranberry and vodka, red wine with steak and mayonnaise and so much better. But half-glug and no sips.

Toronto now

Date: September 30 (9:56:01 pm)
Subject: Toronto now

Dear Hannah,
I want September to be over, despite the already palpable chill in the air. The concrete isn't so wretched in October, the streets are busier than in August or September. Of course, all of the students have settled back in, ruining my carefully constructed, utterly selfish routines, which means that the other academics have also returned. The coffee industry has been preparing itself for our afternoons. The producers of cheap brie are gird-

ing their loins, but I'm sure you're surrounded by academics anyway, and I'm boring you.
Love,
R.

Date: October 1 (5:45:15 pm)
Subject: re: Toronto now

Dear Ray,
None of the women in the apartment are academics. They're all doing the program, like me, to grow Jewishly. Unlike me, however, they all went to Ivy League schools. When a few men from the program came over to visit, it seemed to be the only subject of conversation. They make such a naked display of educational qualifications here. When they asked me where I went to school, I just said "Canada" and we were all content to leave it at that.
Love,
H.

Date: October 3 (9:12:28 am)
Subject: re: re: Toronto now

Tell me about school.
Love,
R.

Date: October 3 (7:22:44 pm)
Subject: re: re: re: Toronto now

Dear Ray,
Classes are thrilling. In the morning, we have a lecture from one of the resident scholars or a distinguished guest speaker (Emil Fackenheim next week—I'm atwitter with excitement) then, after lunch, we have havruta learning, which is new to me. We separate in pairs and discuss the texts, and a rabbi wanders around the room answering any questions that crop up. We have already chosen partners for the whole year—mine is Jenn, that woman I told you about—and we take one line of Torah and discuss it with our partners. It is a brilliant way to learn. I say one line, but we have spent most of our time so far on the first word. A week, in fact, and we have farther to go into this one word.
I love it. And you.
H.

Date: October 4 (3:22:13 pm)
Subject: re: re: re: re: Toronto now

Tell me more.

Jerusalem is a doorway

From the doorway of her delicious room (security being the salt that gives savour to life in a foreign city), Jerusalem is a doorway (being the frontier of its country), and it looks out on eternity (God, Allah, Hashem) and the perfectly plain and ugly day (pimply religious crazies, tourists, boys playing in dirt, cats and lizards, pizza stands, trash).

The day arrives when the rosh yeshiva is scheduled to give some remarks to the students. The lecture hall is noisier than usual, buzzing with expectation at his approach, and even the other professors and rabbis are smiling, attuned to the intensity of the students' anticipation. Under the fold-out desk, Deborah squeezes Hannah's fingers.

Striding to the platform, palm to his wrinkled forehead, Jack Katz appears befuddled, in his own world, unseeing behind his sharp green eyes. Only when he is at the podium does his remarkable height become clear. The lectern reaches a little above his waist. Waving a hand across his hair, he accidentally knocks his kipah to the ground. He stoops to pick it up, kisses it, and places it back on his head, but absently, not thinking about what he's doing.

"Silence, please," he says, his gaze moving from below the feet of his audience to above their heads. "Children, silence," he says. With a louder "Silence, silence," the noise in the auditorium ceases.

His warm voice fills the space like the odour of vanilla bread.

"And so, to conclude, but without making a conclusion, I would like you to remember two

fundamental concepts of Jewish study as you
undertake this journey.

"The first is that there is no end to debate and
that solving the problem, coming to a conclusion,
arriving at a certainty, should not be your goals.
Those goals are antithetical to this undertaking.

"The second is a story, or a sentence really, that
may answer for the first, or it may partially explain
the first. Rabbi Eliezer said to Rabbi Akiba, 'I took
from my masters what a dog takes when it laps the
sea, and my students took from me only what the
tip of a brush takes from a pot of paint.' The goal
is not mastery; it is hesitant, humble and partial
recovery. You may take from the learned rabbis a
little less loss, a pocketful of anti-destruction, but
never the whole. Even when we are studying, time
always makes us stupider.

"My hope for all of you is that you will become
less stupider over the course of this year."

After the applause
dies down

Hannah says, "That was . . ."

"Wonderful?" Deborah offers.

"Miraculous," Hannah corrects.

Deborah smiles. "Don't even get me started."

Hannah, Deborah and
Jenn go shopping
for clothes

In the dim mall outlet, which smells of mothballs
and cabbage, the three women take over a small
curtained change room. The clothes are indistin-
guishable by shape, making their bodies' differ-
ences more apparent. Deborah's dark eyes and
long limbs, browned by the desert, appear at first
glance like a Sabra's, Sephardic anyhow. Jenn is

smaller, with bad skin and curves. They are already almost friends. "Let's go up to Haifa this weekend. Who will go to Haifa with me?" Deborah says.

"Not me. Niklas is coming in this weekend and we'll need alone time." Giggling like girls.

"I'm up for it," Hannah says.

Hannah pulls aside the curtain of the change room to display herself in the standard outfit: a crisp white blouse to her wrists, a black skirt to her ankles. She looks frum (pious). Jenn speaks after they've all watched her turn in the mirror. "I can't say I approve, but it meets the case. You think, Deborah?"

Deborah shrugs. "Put some pearls on, you got pearls? No? Buy some fake pearls and a panier. Everything's good. Get three sets."

"I'm going to get four. Four sets of the skirt and blouse," Hannah says.

"You'll need them in Haifa. Now you, Jenn."

Jenn stands up and asks, "Anyone know the word for 'size' in Hebrew?"

Dismissive, tough—can-you-believe-it, I-practically-lost-it, now-I'm-not-perfect-but—cynical and sentimental—what-school-did-he-go-to—judgmental and vulnerable, the burnished skin and nervous twitches. Under the surface, they're seventy-year-old grandmothers inhaling raspy cigarettes and commentary together. Hannah loves it.

Not princesses

Date: October 6 (8:08:16 pm)
Subject: Feeling at home with myself

Dearest Ray,
As for feeling at home in Judaism, like I planned,
I read in that Friedman book that Israel is the
worst possible place to deal with your Jewish iden-
tity. There are Ashkenazic Jews from Eastern
Europe who have contempt for the Sephardic Jews
from the Arab world, both of whom have con-
tempt for the Ethiopian and Russian Jews. There
are the Druze, who are for us. There are the
Palestinians. There are the ultra-Orthodox in
Polish gear from the nineteenth century in the
middle of the fucking desert and there are the
Sabras who lounge on the beaches and are so
Mediterranean they could be out of Ovid.
Confusion still reigns.

I have something else to confess.

I miss eating with you. Making love, I also
miss. To say that is an understatement would be
an understatement. Satisfy me another way.
SEND ME MAGAZINES. *The New Yorker* costs six
dollars U.S., and I need a *People* fix too.
I won't forget this: I love you.
H.

Date: October 7 (10:15:02 am)
Subject: re: Feeling at home with myself

Dear Hannah,
Since I spend good chunks of every week in the

mag shop, it will be pleasant to satisfy you in this regard. Nice to buy something, too.

It's funny. Ashkenazi, Sephardi, Ethiopians, Russians, Arabs, Poles. Sounds a bit like Toronto, but confusion admits no limits to its dominion, I guess. If you know where to look, I bet there's an Ethiopian-Russian-Polish-Jewish-Arabs of Toronto Society, or ERPJATS for short. Maybe in two generations.
Love,
R.

After the Wall, the Sepulchre, the Dome of the Rock, there's only the heat to see, the streets consuming it as a plant turns light into itself. In the evening, the cool of the air is the day left over. In the morning, the cool is a night remnant. The Old City of Jerusalem is an eye looking straight up, but sometimes you just want to smoke, and it's enough. To get to the Institute, Deborah and Hannah pass a garden where ultra-Orthodox girls sit in the shade reciting memorized psalms. In the evening, after school and a light supper, Hannah lights a cigarette and takes notes. Burnt raisins mixed with corrupt hazelnut toffee mixed with ash resonance of sweaty lips mixed with blue-yellow myrrh gum. Yum.

Habits forming

"Build a fence around the law"—key—This is why families in Mea Sharim have four sets of dishes—four dishwashers for the wealthy—Deborah told me that in some ultra-Orthodox neighbourhoods

Hannah's notes on rabbinic Judaism

the prohibition on saying the name of God is so strong they won't say "ginger ale"—cause Ale is too close to Al—say "ginger cale" instead—deeper I go more methodical more crazy it seems— "Build a fence around the law"—Chapter 1:1, Pirke Avot—"Be deliberate in judgment, raise up many disciples, and build a fence around the law"—To protect Torah—It is this fence I'm passing in and out of this year—like a spy—double double agent

Hannah thinks about God

God. Whatever the Name. And there's God bundled up inside all the word fabrics of these Jewish texts. God of the Jews. Bright illumination. Shadow-making God, too, in addition to His attributes. Wonder of the Holy Name.

This is Deborah

On the dusty salt-stained road to Haifa, the bus is so full that Deborah and Hannah have to squeeze together in the very rear, where they are rattled and jolted and tossed by the driver's radical approach to curves. Deborah must stay perfectly still, focusing on the far distance. "So I don't puke," she says. At the curiously antiseptic and rundown hostel, she argues in fluid, familiar Hebrew with the man at the front desk, the language passing too fast for Hannah to catch more than isolated words and phrases, but in half an hour they have the best room there for ten shekels less than the price posted. Once settled, Deborah takes a bottle of vodka from her bag and pours for them both into plastic bathroom cups. Then they talk for a week. Deborah's face, when she listens, is almost too relaxed, her lips slightly parted, her lids half-drawn, but mostly Hannah does the listening.

Deborah was raised in a brownstone building on the Upper West Side of Manhattan.

She was a virgin until the age of twenty-two.

Her elder sister is a country club wife in Westchester who wept with joy at her baby shower when she received a fifteen-hundred-dollar stroller.

Deborah was in the sixtieth percentile for the LSATs, and won't be going to law school. But she sees it as a blessing.

In college, she was so weight obsessed that, for a few months, she would boil skim milk and spoon the scum off the top.

She was once fitted for a diaphragm, but found the experience so heinous she threw out the prescription. The pill makes her break out in pimples, but she's trying a new brand.

She found out three months ago that her best friend in grade six—they long ago lost touch—killed herself at twenty-three by slashing her wrists in the bathtub.

Her family is not very Jewish. They had Christmas trees. They are completely freaked that she is at yeshiva. Studying in Israel is classic rebellion, Deborah knows it.

Hannah keeps Raymond's existence to herself. With Deborah, the sweetness of new friendship, eager, even greedy, reminds Hannah of the nights she told Raymond that they shouldn't be talking, but to Deborah she doesn't mention the similarity.

This is not Hannah

She doesn't mention that at that moment, while they are on vacation from their yeshiva, a goyish week-long stand may well be sitting down to write her.

Date: October 10 (7:28:21 pm)
Subject: Where are you?

Dear Hannah,
My supervisor just cancelled our regular monthly meeting at the last minute, and so, lacking my usual ordeal, I went to the Fisher library to have a look at their early editions of the AOM. So beautiful and tender holding those books in my hands. I'll have to go back.

By the way, where are you?
Love,
R.

Date: October 13 (7:46:18 pm)
Subject: Haifa

Baby,
I do have an excuse for not writing you this past week. Deborah and I went on a run up to Haifa, which is north of Tel Aviv on the coast. We were there for six days. Sorry.

Now I will tell you about Haifa. I am settled. I have my coffee and my muffin.

In this country, even a small city like Haifa has a temple in it. Baha'i. This religion takes the weirdness of all three faiths and combines them into one fucked fourth. It has a whack of a temple on a big downtown hill. Deborah and I were very impressed and very bored. The beach did not interest us either. We had had too much of that already. So we spent the larger part of the holiday in our hotel room reading, drinking vodka and talking too much. An intellectual spa.

Things are starting to click in the Jewish identity department, but just starting. At the very least, I have realized that I'll never know all the rules, or all the interpretations, since no one does except the huge rabbis. I had an odd sensation today: I couldn't wait to get back to class. I cannot recall ever feeling that way about anything programmed.

On the bus back from Haifa, the driver was playing the radio and everyone was humming along loudly, Deborah too. It was a song about Rabin. Imagine a whole busload of strangers singing a song to a dead politician.

I'm exhausted. I cannot wait to hop into bed.
Love you,
H.

Cast the half-weight of the duvet to the feet, already-drawn curtains, smooth out cotton sleep, cool sheet, sleep, and fade, fade into Bolivian sheets. In my own cool space, home again home again home.

Hannah slips into bed

Instead of the word God, the apartment women only say Hashem, "the Name," and, after a month among them, Hannah finds the word God too

The apartment

naked to utter with an open mouth. Several evenings a week, the women bring home fellow students, and the kitchen fills with political dispute, laughter, religious expostulation, life story confession, and also the usual constant low-grade premarital is-he-the-one sexual tension. Everyone seems to know everything about everyone in a flash. The only distasteful element to Hannah is the competitive Jewishness in the group, each member striving to be more committed and earnest than the next.

Hannah remembers Raymond Not surrendered to the surroundings, because I have and had goyish Toronto Raymond in my bed, cooler than these righteous fucks. The long talks in the bed about Nova Scotia, and Enigma Lake, and drugs. Finishing the last of the Sturplother pot, then sliding into flat-lightning, multicultural, unrighteous sheets, then a walk by the lakeshore or a dinner. Yes, that was nice.

Hannah remembers herself Two months ago, I was packing and I'd never heard of Raymond. I'd never pondered the hermeneutics of exile, or the radical messianic condition of modern Judaism, or seen men praying with chickens before. How did it happen? Went to a party. Took a plane. Fell into bed and rose up in a plane.

Date: October 21 (1:02:31 pm)
Subject: Funny experience

Dear Hannah,
I had a funny experience today, at one of the departmental stand-n-stares. These things are boring with
an over-the-top, operatic boredom. A mature student, intellectual hobbyist really, asked me if I was
single. (A truly desperate daughter or something.)
    "No, I'm not single."
    "Oh."
    "I'm dating a woman in a yeshiva in Jerusalem."
    Blank, mystified stares all around.
Love you,
R.

Date: October 21 (8:04:29 pm)
Subject: re: Funny experience

Funny. Imagine what it's like being inside the
yeshiva and saying you're dating a goy. You really
are an expert on love melancholy, aren't you?
Love,
H.

Date: October 21 (1:09:04 pm)
Subject: re: re: Funny experience

No, I'm an expert on an expert on love melancholy.
But I thought your fellow students were young.
Love,
R.

Date: October 21 (8:15:26 pm)
Subject: re: re: re: Funny experience

Yeah, but still religious.

Date: October 21 (1:28:21 pm)
Subject: re: re: re: re: Funny experience

Blessed art thou in the Holy Land with new friends to surprise and delight you. If I may ask a very Christian question: have you made any plans about Christmas? Return, possibly? Toronto in the depths of winter, I know, is just so tempting.

I feel like a war bride or something.
Your goyish lover,
Raymond

Rabbi Katz on the Wall

The rustle of notes after Rabbi Katz's lecture on idolatry is sensual autumn to the seasons of the mind, but Hannah's curiosity is sempiternal. Hannah collects her things, tells Deborah not to wait up, and stands in line while Rabbi Katz responds to questions about the Malachites and Zoroastrianism. After fifteen minutes of intent listening, the other questioners leave with their answers.

"Yes, you have a question," the rabbi says, cramming his lecture notes into an already overstuffed briefcase.

"I just wanted to ask you about the Wall."

"Yes?"

"I just wanted to know why it isn't considered idolatrous to pray to a wall."

"Yes," he affirms so forcefully that the lecture hall reverberates in its emptiness. "How is this Jewish? Bowing to a wall? This is not Jewish. Good question. Why bow down to a stone? This is not God. This is not Jewish. Good question."

He is beaming with pleasure.

"My name is Jack," he says.

It had to happen sometime, Hannah thinks, amazing it didn't happen in Haifa. She lights a cigarette, even though they're in the bathroom. "Raymond. WASP. Blond hair and blue eyes. I swear if the community at the Institute ever saw him they'd shit, like with Niklas. I don't really even know him. The week before I came here, I picked him up, which was the best week of my life. Just sex and food. But we're still e-mailing, and I've told him I love him, and he's told me that he loves me, so I guess . . ."

Deborah asks about this guy Hannah's being so quiet about

"Hold on a minute. You'd never met him before?" Deborah asks, turning away from the mirror.

"No."

"Never met him, like, at a party or something?"

"I never knew anyone he knew."

"Wow."

"Wow. Yes. But we're still e-mailing."

"Fuck, Hannah. That's fabulous. You're fabulous." Deborah returns to the mirror, licks the tip of her pinky and smooths her brow.

"And there was this . . . you know what? Never mind. I miss him, though. I do miss him."

Hannah knocks an ash into the sink, shrugs, relieved that Deborah at least won't judge. But she does not mention the dark garden where they met, which was lit with candles in glass orbs, or his face as he held a fish at the end of a line, a bass that he caught again the next day. Hannah doesn't mention how he stood in the doorway, leaning against the frame, crying. Enigma Lake.

Dinner party

Date: October 25 (11:33:37 pm)
Subject: Dinner party

Dear Raymond,
There is something fucking fabulous about being surrounded just by Jews, for once. Perhaps in a few months it will seem like less of a miracle. I am finally accustoming myself to the ritual of Shabbat: where to put the candles, when to start the hand-washing, how to recite the blessings. I am beginning to know all those rules about Judaism that I didn't know I wanted to know.

The wine (non-kosher, thanks God) has gone to my head. Tomorrow I will be hungover. But I've been talking far too much about myself, and our correspondence is becoming one-sided. Tell me about your work. You never did explain to me what exactly you're writing your dissertation on. I miss you.
Lots of love,
H.

Date: October 25 (5:21:11 pm)
Subject: re: Dinner party

Hannah,
I think it would be decidedly unjust to poor, hungover you to discuss dissertations. Cruel and unusual punishment.

Wait a minute. I've figured out your little plan now: you worry that, what with the ginormous quantities of booze you've consumed, you won't be able to sleep during the next bit of day, so you've had me write down my thesis to give yourself napping material. Surely, Hannah, there must be a technical manual lying around your apartment.
Love,
Raymond

Date: October 27 (5:41:51 pm)
Subject: re: re: Dinner party

Raymond,
There's no way you're getting out of it that easily. I've told you one thing after another about my loopy religious program, and now it's your chance to return the favour.
Love,
H.

Date: October 29 (3:31:57 pm)
Subject: re: re: re: Dinner party

Dear Hannah,
Since you have asked, I will write down the lies I am telling myself this week about how I am going to write a dissertation and you can peruse them after your tea and eggs tomorrow morning (or is that now? I can never figure that out).

I was going to write about the pastoral and its relationship to technology in Donne, Bacon, Browne, Burton and Cowley, but that is no longer feasible, by which I mean it would be too much work. So now I am writing a Single Author Dissertation (SAD) just on Burton, specifically on the third part of *Anatomy of Melancholy,* which deals with love melancholy. Are you paying attention? A very basic reading and comparative textual analysis of the five editions published during his lifetime. Is that you snoring across the ocean? Perhaps this will not be enough, in which case I'll come up with more. Must discuss with supervisor, something I keep putting off.

That's enough.
Love,
R.

Date: October 31 (9:12:41 pm)
Subject: re: re: re: re: Dinner party

Your thesis sounds by no means boring. That said, I'm not sure I understand it. It must be the same

for you with all this wacky Judaica.
Love,
H.

Hannah and Jenn pause over the line for several minutes: "Take now your son, your only son, the one you love, Yitzhak." The rest of the room, filled as it is with havruta partners, rumbles gently with debate. "Hold on," Jenn says, "why all this junk?"

"Take now your son, your only son, the one you love, Yitzhak"

"Synonyms," Hannah offers.

"Why, though?"

Hannah muses. "Take *Beowulf*. Take the *Iliad*. You get these epics that come out of oral tradition. The oral poet needs new ways of saying 'king,' so he says 'wonderful king,' 'giver of rings,' a whole bunch of them."

"But Hannah, this isn't oral literature. It's texts. It's all books."

"Must have been oral at one point."

"Been altered, Hannah. Let's take a look at the line again."

"'Take now your son, your only son, the one you love, Yitzhak.' Well, we do need to know all this stuff. It matters that the sacrifice is a son, an only son and beloved."

"Fine. Say, 'Take your beloved only son Isaac. Cuts out the garbage."

"You're right. He could have been more concise."

"And He tends to be concise. What does Rashi say?"

Hannah flips through the books beside her bookstand. "Quote: 'Your son. When Abraham heard this, he said to Him, "I have two sons." God said to him, "Your only one." Abraham said to Him, "This one is the 'only one' of his mother, and this other one is the 'only one' of his mother." God said to him, "Whom you love." Abraham said to Him, "I love both of them." God said, "Isaac." And why did He not reveal to him that it was Isaac from the start? So as not to suddenly confuse him, lest his mind become disoriented, and addled.' Unquote."

Jenn is mute, leaning back in her chair with folded arms, genuinely awed. "Now that is an answer."

Hannah sees Jenn at the gate

Niklas hovering for Jenn at the Institute door. Thanks God, she too has a goyish man, too nervous even to enter the yeshiva lobby, for it redeems Raymond and Hannah, yes. Less shame for me. She is a woman and proud. She will read whatever moves her. I will sleep with whomever I love.

Dinner party resumed

Date: November 1 (8:33:57 pm)
Subject: re: re: re: re: re: Dinner party

Dear Hannah,
No, no, no, I love it. Words are serious there. Books are holy. I admire it no end, and I'm more than a little jealous—it's so the opposite of my daily rounds of empty-handed library visits. I mean, there's still Burton, who is a delight, but I have to wait around in a huge crowd of pseuds to have a word with the man. The system there

seems infinitely more efficient and pleasurable. I wonder if it is somehow transferable to university life here. That ancient method has got to work better than our foul and lonely rule by committees of elders. But I'm getting bitter here.
Love you, and sleep well.
Raymond

Date: November 3 (7:04:44 pm)
Subject: re: re: re: re: re: re: Dinner party

Ray,
Noticed how our affair is hingeing on weird, strangely orchestrated words? Burton and Talmud. Despite all the memories I'm gathering, filling me up, our week together is still absolutely clear.
I love you,
Hannah

Deborah joins the crowd of women, leans her head against the stone, and whispers into a crack. She prays earnestly, her eyes closed. There is no reserve, no irony or need for it.

"You looked intense there, Deborah."

"It's the Wall," she says, as a kind of explanation. For Hannah, the Wall needs more explanation than that. Should she be moved just by putting her hand against a massy chunk of stone? The whole glow of the rugged stone is others' touch or sun or God or all. And it's just stone.

Deborah and Hannah go to the Wall

Jews have no Chartres Cathedral. They have no Al-Aqsa mosque. The most important Jewish building in the world is a ruined wall, and the best Jewish building is the model the messianists have made out of cardboard and balsam for the day when they can rebuild the temple. And perhaps Jewish buildings will be beautiful when the Messiah does come, but in the unredeemed world there are ornate candlesticks. There are exquisite cups for terrible wine, and spice boxes so elaborate and perfect they make profane time sweet. There are silver paperweight Jerusalems you can hold in your hand.

Inside the box, which cost sixty dollars to send, there is a short note from her non-Jewish unbeliever lover. "You asked, XO, Raymond." *The New Yorker, Atlantic Monthly, People, Harper's, Glamour, Cosmopolitan:* for the next few weeks, Hannah will be everyone's good friend for sharing glossy images of the secular North American life that her non-Jew lover sent from Canada.

Let's pretend—it's so Christian to think of an afterlife but that's the Diaspora—let me pretend that my life is foreseen. A Jewish woman in an attic apartment in Rosedale, in Toronto, in the twentieth century. Explorer of bodies, she ended up falling in love, in a week, with a goy. Then she came to Jerusalem, and fell in love with Judaism, with the city of it and Rabbi Katz. Okay. That's the synopsis. Barest outline. From it, can we see where the story tends? Homeland or exile? Which one is Israel, which one Diaspora?

"I guess my question is, would Israel be here with-out the Diaspora?" Hannah asks.

Rabbi Katz on Diaspora dreams

Rabbi Katz cradles his tense brow in a measured hand. The group clustered around the lectern falls silent. At length, he replies with a question.

"Hannah, where are you from?"

"Toronto."

"Toronto?"

"Yes."

"Well, that's a nice city. Plenty of Jews, too. Tell me, Hannah, are you here now because you were born there?"

The rest of the group looks to her for an answer. The question is illegitimate, but she can-not say so, she doesn't want to, so she refrains from answering.

"Let me tell you a story about the moment I knew I was going to be a rabbi." Murmurs of excitement for the future gossip. "In my twen-ties, I was a lobster fisherman in Maine. Now that is the deep Diaspora. Lobster fishing. But a good life, clean, the sea air. One day, I was in port, and I liked to drink Campari with soda then. I was having a Campari and soda in Rockland, Maine, and I wondered if the Campari was kosher. And I asked for the bottle so I could see if it had a marker.

"That's it. Now I'm the head of this yeshiva. You work it out."

Date: November 14 (8:35:35 pm)
Subject: Crazy

Dear Hannah,
It occurred to me this afternoon that we will have spent 97.5% of our time together in different cities when we see each other again. This thought is so ridiculous it makes me laugh and chills me.
Your,
Raymond

Date: November 15 (6:32:04 pm)
Subject: re: Crazy

Only six more months. Not that long when you think about it.

Date: November 15 (7:16:59 pm)
Subject: re: re: Crazy

Dear Hannah,
Oh I know. It's just sometimes, when I'm locked in the concrete Robarts box, I wonder where you are.

Given any more thought to the annual Mass for the celebration of the birth of our Lord and Saviour Jesus Christ? Coming home with Santy Claus? I miss you terribly as you can see.

Perhaps you have ventured for a little run up to the Temple Mount or the Holy Sepulchre. I'll imagine you in both places as I walk home and drift off to slumber.

Your lover,

R.

With the Torah in her hand, Hannah is smoking on her porch, thinking about what she's falling for.

But Hannah is on her porch

The Book is so very rich and handsome and, on Sunday, Deborah, Jenn and I will walk together through the city, under the canopies of the stores' eves, past the highways to the sprawling strip mall and the Institute, to study it.

What I'm falling for

"As for the winter holidays, I don't think anyone is leaving," Deborah says, "except for Marcia, who came to a yeshiva and doesn't like to read. Don't get me started. I wonder if she'll even come back. I suppose she will. She paid the full year's tuition already."

Plans for Hanukkah

"How do you know that?"

"Jenn told me. What I want to know is where Jenn gets this stuff. She has the best info. She must know somebody in the registrar's office. Of course, you're the teacher's pet now."

Hannah ignores the backhanded flattery, which brightens her nevertheless. "Jenn protects her sources."

"Fair enough. Jesus Christ, Hannah. Loshen hora, loshen hora. We should be talking about the rabbis or something."

Hannah considers this. "Have you ever noticed with Rick, how he leaves the room when people start gossiping now?"

"Yeah. Weird. Sexy guy, though."

"You know, I think we should have a Hanukkah party here. I think we should have it in the apartment. Everybody would be into it, don't you think?" Deborah's eyes have already lit up.

Planning
Date: November 21 (6:43:09 pm)
Subject: Planning

Raymond,
Being at a Jewish institute, the program does not break for Christmas. Besides, the only flight I could afford back to Toronto would leave me two weeks out of the program. I can't do that. Sorry.
I am very sorry.
I love you.
H.

Date: November 22 (4:14:05 pm)
Subject: re: Planning

Dear Hannah,
Won't say that doesn't hurt. Isn't there a Chanukah (sp?) break? Something? Anything?
Love,
R.

Date: November 25 (5:12:51 pm)
Subject: re: re: Planning

Hanukkah just isn't a big enough holiday to justify
a break. Please don't make me feel guilty about
this, because I just can't afford the two thousand
dollars that a trip would cost. Believe me when I
tell you that I want it as much as you do.
Love,
H.

It's not the white city, not the learning, not even   What she's falling for
the communities and the entitlements they estab-
lish; not, to go deeper, the rituals, the physical
practices that are embraces to God written out in
a manual. It's the curious tales of curious Jews, of
which she is one.

A man was caught outside the eruv as the sun   Curious tales of
curious Jews
went down on Shabbos. His bus was caught in
traffic, and he was forced to step out twenty-five
blocks from his stop. He would have to walk
home, transportation was forbidden, but there
was a further problem: he couldn't carry the
challah he had with him outside of the eruv after
sundown. It was forbidden. And so he was faced
with a decision: either throw away the bread,
which was necessary for the meal, or stay put.
Then he remembered another law, one to protect
the kitchen from sacrilege: it is permitted to take
three steps carrying a loaf of bread. There was the
solution. For twenty-five blocks, he took three

steps carrying the loaf, then put it down, picked it up, took another three steps, and so went on.

Another curious Jew, Eliezer, called the walls to witness that he was right in his dispute with Joshua, an argument concerning the purity of ovens. A river ran backwards for him. A tree uprooted itself, and finally a voice from heaven called out that Eliezer had judged properly. The walls leaned, but did not collapse. Joshua pointed out that miracles should never decide questions of real importance, such as the meaning of the Torah. God had already had his say. Because Eliezer was right, but proven only by means of heaven, he was declared anathema.

Hannah always attends her apartment's Shabbat dinner, where they follow all the commandments, and after the meal seriously discuss the meaning of the rabbis and prophets. But the moment Hannah excuses herself, she breaks all the prohibitions. She lights a cigarette and heads to the Internet café to write a good, long, electronic letter to Raymond.

Hannah hears the silence of Shabbat

Program

Date: November 29 (10:36:58 pm)
Subject: Program

Dearest Raymond,
I'm just going to clear my head if you don't mind, which I know you won't.

I have figured out, for myself, that the most important part of these nine months so far is Jerusalem, being in it, seeing it, knowing what it does to people and what people do to it. Living in a Jewish country, in a Jewish city, has been one of the most important things ever to happen to me. I think at one point I thought I was less of a Jew because I didn't know enough about the laws or customs. Now, even with the little learning I have picked up, with the few prayers that I know how to say, I feel that I am "as Jewish as the next woman."

But Jerusalem is the key. It is hard from here not to think of everything in Toronto as petty. People kill each other here over spaces the size of a living room, or beams in churches that you could barely hang a coat on. The flip side of that intensity is that, when dust shifts here, it matters. You must come and visit, Raymond. If you can come for a month, come for a month.
I love you.
Hannah

Lilith loved Adam, and she wanted his love in full, in the Edenic way where each is servant of the other. Equality was not in Adam's mind, nor God's, and after a series of fruitless discussions, Lilith ran off to the Red Sea, and would never have her long hair brought back to the earthly garden.

Another curious lover, Casanova, began his day with fifty oysters to prepare himself for an afternoon's display of womanflesh. Before him, Abelard and Eloise turned absence into the substance of their fever, and grew old in the expectation of no reward.

Raymond and Hannah poured themselves into light signals fluttering in the space over the Atlantic. They sit at desks taking notes and are lovers.

Hannah's notes on love and history Girl today in class—visiting a friend in the program—sat in on lecture—we were discussing intermarriage—got quite heated—her name was Ruth, I think (Rachel? Rebecca?)—told this story—at her Hebrew school they were asked to recite "intermarriage is the second Holocaust"— whole class of eight-year-olds repeating this phrase over and over—Jenn, because of Niklas, bristled visibly—R. could not be older than 35—I thought of Moses—Moses raised by foreigners— Moses married a non-Jew—So—a) he knows more than anyone why Jews must be Jews—b) he overcompensates for his partial Jewishness—if he was just Jewish he could have bowed to the calf like the rest of them—no—something to prove— must be more Jewish than the Jews—must lead them to Israel

Toronto in December Date: December 7 (9:09:09 am)
Subject: Toronto in December

Dear H,
First big snow happened last night. It's funny how snow doesn't make Toronto white. The whole spectrum from pale straw to charcoal first, then all

96

the other kinds of grey: yellow-grey, blue-grey, beige. I think what I need is Jerusalem. You may come to regret that offer because I am socking away my pennies.

It is snowing so thickly that I must run home before it becomes impossible to leave the library.
Love,
R.

Date: December 9 (10:36:58 pm)
Subject: re: Toronto in December

Dearest Raymond,
At least you are getting your work done. Everything here is devolving into pure social scene. No one except me and a few other geeks care about studying any more. You being here in Jerusalem fills me with joy just thinking about it. Please, please, put aside some money. When I think about Our Week, and try to fuse it with my life in Jerusalem over the past three months, literally my heart starts to beat faster. Put away some money, keep working, come and see me.
Love,
H.

Date: December 11 (10:15:41 am)
Subject: re: re: Toronto in December

Dear Hannah,
I wish I were working. I'm mostly just reading. My apartment is my pied-a-terre. The library is

now my home. Like, I'm starting to know regu-
lars. I have made some progress in the sucking
up department, however. Two profs have asked
me over for Christmas Eve dinner, well in
advance of the season. I think they heard about
my last Christmas Eve, which I spent watching
movies. A movie theatre during Christmas in
Toronto is just like Jerusalem: nothing but Jews
and Arabs.

Your lover,

Ray

White on white — It snows on Jerusalem every now and then.
Everyone comes out to throw snowballs and take
snapshots, tourists in their own country. It covers
both east and west. Mea Sharim is covered, and
the German Colony, and the square in front of the
Wall that used to be full of Arab stalls. When the
snow melts into the streets, the children race
toothpicks in the gutters.

Hannah walks through the snow to the
Institute as it begins to melt, and for the first time
in her life, she's happy it's cold. She can make a
snowball. She can think about the name God,
about Jews and Raymond and home.

Hannah thinks about — I can think God but not say "God." God is Hashem.
the name God — Hashem is "the Name." The Name is infinite, and
the infinite is why snow is falling, December is passing, in the study of Torah, silently and smoothly,
among the chosen people in Jerusalem, and I am
among them.

Molly Shanoff, Zadie, Bubbie, Elsie Rabkov, the About Jews
Spitzes, the Strenns, Jews, Jews, Jews, dry chicken
and bad wine, sometimes raisins in the food.
From the chosen, I may choose. If not the light, a
light among other lights and darknesses: Ethiopia
and Arabia, Yemen, Iraq, India too, and Long
Island, Detroit, Los Angeles, New York. Toronto
and Jerusalem.

Raymond is not a Jew. About Raymond

Toronto or Jerusalem? "This community has About home
become so important to me." Let me say what I
like. If there was an end, it would lead to the book-
home of the Torah and reading it with Jenn at the
Institute. And Raymond, lying in bed in the dark,
wordless, perfect, and the sun comes up in awkward angles from the skylights. That too and more
and more. Remember?

In havruta class, Jenn has chosen "Let down your "Let down your pitcher, I pray you, that I may drink"
pitcher, I pray you, that I may drink" for attention,
and Hannah is fine with that.
"A well. Always a well," Jenn says.
"Better than a bar."
"Better than a bar, true."
"You meet God in the desert and pick up at
wells," Hannah says with a shrug.
"I think Robert Alter said something about this,
but mostly 'cause it keeps getting repeated. Mostly
about that. Holes and sex. Makes sense."
"Near a house. Domestic," Hannah suggests.

"Dark and wet."

"Water of life."

"You lean over to draw up the water."

"Drinking and sex, the two go together. We're all water fetishists. Remember that the next time you're at a water fountain." The rows of students at their table pause to listen to Jenn's laugh.

Rabbi Katz on the Messiah

"There have been many Messiahs, not just Yeshua, and I mean to say, let us not forget that they have all been imagined by Jews, created by Jews. Then rejected by Jews.

"It is not so simple, then, to blame this group or that one. We think them up. We are the original attendants of the Messiahs, and we are also always the ones who are quite sure He has not come.

"We expect Him to come any second, but He has never come. Write that down. Pay attention to the tenses. And have a Merry Christmas."

After lecture

Deborah says, "That's half. Can you believe that this half of study is done?"

"I know," Hannah says.

"The year's half done."

"Don't even get me started."

"I feel like I'm blushing with sadness, you know."

They wait, seated, while their fellow students file out.

Hanukkah

So many people are coming for dinner that they are forced to snake the table through two different rooms, and from any individual seat, half the party is obscured. The hosts agree that this is very New York, especially considering the three tablecloths, each of a different colour, and the china borrowed from the neighbours. Only the plastic water jugs, borrowed from the Institute's storeroom, match.

Guests arrive in staggered blocks, bearing wine and dishes. The conversation rises pitch by pitch until, after a solemn lighting of the candles and a few short prayers, they sit down to the meal. Then silence fills ten minutes while they destroy a few platters of potato kugel and an enormous chunk of sea bass.

Talk is awkwardly limited by the position of the tables, and some guests can eavesdrop on only half a conversation. In Hannah's corner, at a sharp turn in the hall, a woman from Texas, who has the most beautiful curls of strawberry blond hair, explains how she is going to cut them all off when she moves to a settlement at Efrat. "There's a woman there," she says, "who's so holy she finds it hard to go to the bathroom, because it's forbidden to think about Hashem then." Another man, who has an MBA from Harvard, explains why birthday parties aren't Jewish. "In Judaism, we light candles. We don't blow them out."

They drink well into the night, but Hannah doesn't speak much. She imagines the families she could raise with the men in the room. The Jewish babies they could all give her. She listens patiently to the mock-arguments, which spill out from the table into the hall, and eventually from the hall into the street. The women of the apartment insist that cleaning up will take no time at all.

No one used the dreidels laid out on the table, Hannah noticed. In the Hanukkahs of her past, even last year's, spinning the tops had been the entire point of the evening. The gold chocolate coins sprinkled on the tablecloth went untouched too, but this is adulthood. Adulthood is looking at the tops, and remembering, not touching. On the other hand, she has never experienced a Hanukkah so fascinating, a Hanukkah when she had learned so much.

It's 1:12 a.m. by the time Hannah gets to her room. She has waited until this moment to open the package from Raymond. The gift is a bowl covered with Flemish-style drawings of animals and ships. In it are a package of dirt and four narcissus bulbs. Raymond has attached a note:

> Happy Hanukkah (+ Merry X-Mass too). I'm quite sure this little package of dirt and life is highly illegal. But an ecological disaster would barely be noticed there I imagine. Stay safe and warm. Love, Raymond.

She will put the flowers on her desk. The flowers will grow. If anyone asks their origin, she will lie; she will tell them her mother sent them. And now she wishes to be in Toronto, where she could touch him there, Raymond. What was that?

Deborah comes into the room, looks over the note, the gift, kisses Hannah's forehead, and puts her to bed.

When the sun rises, there will be a day that reaches out, only one. The sky will hold them.

Raymond and Hannah

Date: December 22 (10:36:58 pm)
Subject: I love you

I love you

Raymond,
Despite Hanukkah, the truth is I'm missing you horribly. I'm missing Toronto too, if you can believe it. I even miss, in some part of me, Christmas.
    So much for growing Jewishly.
I love you.
Hannah

Date: December 22 (10:40:19 pm)
Subject: I love you again

And thanks for the gifts.

The roar of diesel fumes and the hawking of the fishmongers; the sawdust floor purveyors are open. The neon in the pornography store signs is flowing. For Hannah, it is the most special Christmas ever exactly because there is nothing special about it. The city goes about its business, Hannah goes to school without remark, and in the evening, after a simple meal, she is pleased to take

Christmas Day

notes without considering the birthday of a crazy preacher somebody else believes in.

Hannah's notes on belief

Key fact—Judaism is about practice—not belief— Like yoga? Like gymnastics? God there as an immutable, infinitely removed cause—how modern—for modern problem about religion is this— mere belief in belief—believe that belief in angels is a good thing but not that angels actually exist— believe in the beauty of paintings, not in the truth of them—that's fine—set a table for the pope, the rabbis and the imams—only possible with hypocrisy—so—my beliefs are confused—if you're not confused, you're not thinking clearly— I do love the kiddush cup, the quiet of the Sabbath—the lighting of candles, the breaking of bread—I can have them both—joy—plus all the craziness of Pascal's wager.

Hannah considers where Raymond's body is

The blink of an eye. Raymond's body. Only four months ago, I touched it, made love to it. The rings on my right hand grazed the contours of his ribs. My left hand grasped the throb. Kissed his face, kissed whatever my face grasped. And I wonder what I've forgotten, wonder what's changed, haven't noticed I've forgotten. What was that? All the different kinds of sex: fuck buddies, one-night stands, platonic lovers, husbands. What was that? I wonder where his body is.

Where Raymond's body is

Raymond's body is breathing the purified air in the reading room of the Thomas Fisher library.

Above him, like the insides of a giant brain, are the coiled, ovoid floors of books, from which a librarian is picking out the second and fifth editions of *Anatomy of Melancholy*, thick with book dust.

Raymond considers books and animals

Sniffing each other, screwing, chewing the best thing we can find, living, seeing, dying, we're animals. *Animal animalis*. Then we have books, beyond our animal selves, we're told. And then here I see a lost cover. There is a title page missing, decorating some wealthy melancholic's study now, words unreadable for the stains. Smell it: ash of a thousand-year burn. Worse than corpses, dead books, lost ones, the ones soaked in muddy water. Books are animals too, fuck it.

Date: January 6 (3:03:33 pm)
Subject: Happy new year

Happy new year

Raymond,
New Year's was quiet, just like I like it. Deborah and I shared a bottle of cheap champagne, and decided the narcissus plants will be our symbol of the upcoming year. They are fragile but hardy and may even survive my ash thumb.
I love you.
Hannah

Date: January 6 (11:58:47 am)
Subject: re: Happy new year

Dear Hannah,
I've just come from the Fisher rare book room where I had my religious experience for the day. They had beautiful copies of the AOM, and I troubled the librarians to bring me the second and fifth editions. I have to say that old books do it for me. I love their smell. I love their weight and the grittiness of their survival. I love having their dust on my hands. Monasteries in Europe would sometimes import soil from Jerusalem to cover their floors. Book dust is that holy, I think sometimes.

As for the paper-whites, those things survive on nothing and thrive on a little water, so you shouldn't worry. I don't think you even need the dirt.
Love you,
R.

Date: January 6 (7:03:21 pm)
Subject: re: re: Happy new year

Since you're at a computer right this moment, if you are coming to Jerusalem, we should make plans immediately, so I can decide how long I'm going to stay after school ends. Please come. It's been four months since that glorious week. We're getting closer to the 97.5% of the sentence completed.
Love,
H.

Date: January 6 (2:31:21 pm)
Subject: re: re: re: Happy new year

Dear Hannah,
Yes, it's true. We're at 44% or something. Every day works out to a little under half a percent.

I'm still looking into it. The idea is ludicrously attractive to me, but there are money issues and time issues. I am very, very close to finding a way, and will let you know soon, but I must go home now. The library and I have spent too much time together today.
Love you,
Raymond

Built in the mid-sixties and reportedly a cause of several of its architects' suicides, the Robarts Library building is a grotesquerie parodying scholarship: it supposedly imitates a peacock (with a hundred vigilant eyes) but looks more like a turkey. Raymond's routine is formed by this architecture, the elevator down to the Fisher basement for his research into rare books and first editions, the narrow escalator up to the fourth floor for journal articles, the reading room where if he keeps shifting he can always find the perfect quantity of light in the afternoon. A false but persistent legend claims that the architects failed to take into account the weight of the books, and so the library is slowly sinking into the ground.

Robarts Library

The walk home — Raymond is slowly sinking into the ground as he walks away from it.

Raymond walking home — Crunch, crunch, hunched, hunched, in the window of the Korean aesthetician is advertised skin-whitening powder. Powder of book dust. Connection. Winter. And the rape of Proserpine, three or was it four pomegranate seeds, or was it six, hope and so lonely in his basement apartment, god of the underworld, he, Plutonic.

Pigeons in Toronto — In the evening, in the low and early cold shadows, a huge shimmering flock of pigeons begins to circle over Toronto. The pigeons don't understand where they are, searching for a place to settle over the low squat buildings, between the towers, above the homes and markets. It all looks the same to them. They circle over Chinese, Italian, WASP, Portuguese, Vietnamese, Korean, Pakistani, Caribbean neighbourhoods, too stupid to tell the difference.

Raymond's basement apartment — Raymond's apartment is just as you would expect for a young man who frequently returns after midnight and leaves before eight in the morning. Glasses glisten in smudgy piles on every surface. The sheets are a curled question mark on his bed. Books squat broken-backed or spread out on each other over the floor. Luxury is a bottle of whisky, from which he takes a nip before sleep to consider the broader context of the university.

The most obvious feature of the university, when considered within an urban context, is that it is the location of the books. Only slightly less obvious is the fact that the social function of the university is to provide people just ending adolescence with a place for open-ended sexual intercourse. The libraries of a university awe all private book collections. Similarly, the sexual life of the university, in both quantity and intensity of focus, puts to shame the sexual lives that surround it. Books and sex: the university concentrates what mature men and women dip into only when time and occasion permit.

Raymond considers the broader context of the university

But what eludes us is the co-incidence of books and sex. Why is the site for the concentration (or disposal) the same? Is it that sex and books are the substance of youth and must be, then, simultaneously contained?

Jerk off, read a chapter, go to sleep. Night after night.

Date: January 11 (6:14:23 pm)
Subject: Dates and package

Dates and package

Raymond,
It's decided that I am now definitely leaving Israel on May 29. There may be seats still left on that flight, so perhaps you can join me. It doesn't matter so much if I'm in school during the day while you are here, I think, because you will need time to explore the city alone. Maybe we will go away for little weekend trips?

Has a certain box arrived?
Love,
Hannah

Date: January 13 (10:14:14 am)
Subject: re: Dates and package

Hannah,
Opened your e-mail, read the line about a certain
package arriving, went straight to the post office,
and there it was. Mr. Postman brought out a
fancy little box from Jerusalem. It is the perfect
gift, Hannah. A little silver Jerusalem. I spent
last night putting it in different places around
my apartment. Tried putting it on a shelf with
my photographs, but it kind of faded into the
background there. Thought about putting it on
the phone table where I could see it every day,
but what would I do with it? Fidget while I make
calls? I don't make any phone calls. No good. In
the end, I made it my paperweight. Maybe that's
what it's actually intended to be. The thing looks
like a village nestled in a mountain or a valley
wherever I put it down on my paper-covered
desk. A reminder of you among all this
bookjunk.
    Thank you.
Best regards,
Ray

Date: January 14 (5:18:29 pm)
Subject: re: re: Dates and package

"Best regards"!!?? Look over that last message.
Love,
H.

Date: January 14 (5:45:07 pm)
Subject: re: re: re: Dates and package

I'm so sorry. These sign-offs can get to be such a habitual thing. I'm just hoping I didn't sign off to my supervisor "Love, Ray." I suppose she'll tell me when I see her later this week at the coffee hour. I will get it right this time:
I love you,
Raymond

Date: January 15 (7:11:51 pm)
Subject: re: re: re: re: Dates and package

That's better. And yes, it is a paperweight.
Love,
H.

A week after undergraduate classes have recom- **Term starts**
menced, the traditional rounds of departmental get-togethers for graduate students and faculty begin. Raymond goes in order to remind his supervisor of his existence.

The casual coffee hour takes place in the close, low-ceilinged hallway of the administrative offices.

There being no chairs, the forty or so participants hover in uncomfortable, standing cliques. The food matches the atmosphere: cheap acidic coffee and expensive English biscuits, gummy brie and flaccid grapes on plastic platters. Raymond nibbles whatever is closest, examining the room with quick half-glances, careful to avoid conversation.

Academic conversation

"Hey Raymond, how are you?"

"Hi, [insert name here, if not forgotten]. Fine. Great."

"How's your work going?"

"I'm working on *Anatomy of Melancholy* these days. Going well. And you? How are you doing?"

"I'm working on [insert text or author or period or genre] and it's going all right."

"Great."

"Excuse me, I think I see [insert other graduate student's name]."

Raymond has this conversation half a dozen times with fellow students: a morose Chaucerian, a Derridean Donne scholar, a critic and analyst of Western-themed pornography novels from the nineteenth century, two Shakespeareans who always travel as a pair, and a British visiting scholar of a minor Jamaican poet.

Professors and their nicknames

The alcoholic golfer. A heavyweight priest called the Anglican Mass. Dr. Fidget. (Some of these professorial nicknames are Raymond's own, others are general but he has forgotten their provenances.) Queen WASP. Snaggletooth. Crazy Jane (Raymond's supervisor, so called because she always wears clashing clothes, plaid pants with an argyle top, for example, or a man's suit jacket with a miniskirt). The Plodder. The Lady Who Speaks with the Squirrels.

Where is she? Where is she? Where is Crazy Jane? Scanning the room for Crazy Jane

Crazy Jane passes him like a minor starlet at an advance screening. "Raymond, how are you? But I can't talk now. See you when? February. Fabulous. February." Gone. Successful event

Raymond smiles and waves at her turned back, thinking that this couldn't have worked out better. He can now finish his grape and brie in peace, wash them down with a half-styrofoam cup of white wine, acknowledge the half-nods, and then leave, escaping into twenty-below-zero. Tomorrow he will check for messages from Jerusalem.

Date: January 16 (9:23:13 pm)
Subject: Rabbi Katz

Rabbi Katz

Ray, have I ever told you about Rabbi Jack Katz?

Date: January 17 (11:11:14 am)
Subject: re: Rabbi Katz

Is Jack a diminutive of Jeremiah or Jephthah or something? Jack doesn't sound very Jewish. Still, tell me all about Rabbi Jack.
Love,
Raymond

Date: January 18 (9:43:53 pm)
Subject: re: re: Rabbi Katz

Dear Raymond,
He was born Jack in Maine, deep, deep Diaspora.
Now he's head of his own yeshiva.

Two nights ago, he invited me over for Shabbat dinner with his family, which is kind of a big deal. Everyone was jealous, anyway, mostly because I got to see the inside of his house, and it was quite amazing. There were so many commentaries on the shelves, the living room looked like a lawyer's office. Huge strappings of bland homespun food and five beautiful kids. Great songs, none of which I'd heard before. A marvellous Dvar Torah (which is when somebody does a commentary on a bit of the Bible over dinner). It was the quintessential Shabbos, all rabbinical groundedness and family wholeness. I kind of felt like crying in a happy way most of the evening, but I'm sentimental.

It wasn't just that, either. The amazing part was that his bookshelves had Heidegger, Sartre, novels by Ivan Klima, Graham Greene. All I could think was, Here are both worlds, both my worlds. I felt so at home. Of course, after I left, I immediately went to an Internet cafe and wrote you an e-mail, which is so against the rules. But you and I need to be reading, all the time to be reading.
Love you,
H.

When he isn't reading, he's thinking about reading, on the subway, in his apartment, in the
library. When he needs to take notes, the margins
serve him for paper and his lap for a desk.

"There will not be wanting, I presume, one or   Part 3,
other that will much discommend some part of   section 1, member 1.
this Treatise of Love-Melancholy, and object   subsection 1
(which Erasmus in his Preface to Sir Thomas
More suspects of his) that it is too light for a
Divine, too Comical a subject, to speak of Love-
Symptoms, too phantastical, and fit alone for a
wanton Poet, a feeling young love-sick gallant, an
effeminate Courtier, or some such idle person."

A classic Burtonian entrance, this sentence is a
synecdoche for the entire *Anatomy of Melancholy*.
Burton anticipates his critics by moving from
counter-argument to acknowledgement to active
encouragement of the imaginary audience who
would reject love as a subject. The sentence struc-
ture is syntactically and grammatically integrated,
while containing a fourfold thought. A fine balance between chaotic rambling and uncompro-
mising logic poses the phrases in this particular
order. Burton's treatment of love is a poise: intelligence holding back waves of lust and resentment,
the language of the don constraining the dirty
Petrarchan sonneteer, an origami box filled with a
flaming bright coal. Also there is the not minor
point that we actually are a bunch of feeling young
lovesick effeminate idle persons, we students for a
living, myself included. But with Hannah, there

was no reading despite what she just wrote. I remember looking at this very book and asking how I was ever going to look at it again. Then to bed with whisky and flesh, new laughter and the rest. Must go buy that ticket to Jerusalem, City of the Book, where I can stop reading again. And there's my paperweight on the desk, as if I had conjured it.

Silver Date: January 20 (10:32:08 pm)
Subject: Silver

Dear Hannah,
Jack from Maine with five kids and a yeshiva. I can't wait to meet these people. In my silver Jerusalem, you can see houses and churches and so on, and I have spent several hours this morning staring at them. I must see them myself. Betraying my childishness here, but there's this real feeling of power you get from holding a city in your hand. I have procrastinated too long with the tickets. I will go to the travel agent soon. Promise.
Love,
Raymond

Instead of the travel agent Instead, he wanders Toronto the Grey, in the cold, and stops at a bookstore, and a Korean cake shop, and a magazine stand.

Patient comprehension At the Maison de la Presse Internationale, Raymond searches for literature that will please Hannah. She likes *Commentary* magazine. She asked for *Tikkun,* which he has never heard of. A clerk has to help him find it among the religious magazines, alongside titles for Buddhists, Wiccans, liberation theologians. Hannah also wants women's magazines and *The New York Review of Books* and *People.* Already, because of the visit to the religion section, the clerk has suspicions, but Raymond can see that *Cosmopolitan* and *Glamour* have thrown him off track. Experienced in selling all manner of freak magazine to the most minuscule niches in the market, the clerk's reaction to Raymond's purchase is faint, but palpable too. Raymond imagines explaining, justifying himself, saying that they're all for a woman he knew for a week five months ago, but how would that explain or justify at all?

Sitting on the pier reading every last word of the newspaper, what's with that, Hannah? What would Burton say about that? And what would Burton say about the McDonald's on Markham Street I pass every day, the one filled with old people nursing free refills of coffee from six to eleven? The human need for love is so infinite that a ninety-eight-cent coffee can be nurtured for five hours to share a room with other hearts beating. What would Robert have said? Books don't know how old or young you are. Joy and horror. If I can spin it into a longer bit.

Raymond thinks of something to write Hannah

"So did those three gentlewomen, in Balthasar Castilio, fall in love with a young man, whom they

Part 3, section 2, member 2, subsection 2

117

never knew, but only heard him commended: or by reading of a letter; for there is grace commeth from hearing, as a moral philosopher informeth us, as well as from sight; and the species of love are received into the phantasy by relation alone; both senses affect. Sometimes we love those that are absent, saith Philostratus, and gives instance in his friend Athenodorus, that lov'd a maid at Corinth whom he never saw; we see with the eyes of our understanding."

The core of Burton can be found in the casual, unsystematic corners of his work. The miscellany chapters, where he purports to sweep up the unused refuse of his research, are always the most illuminating. The autobiographical angle—the lonely, isolated scholar recovering endless love tales—opens into a broader revelation: the fantasy of all writers that people will fall in love by reading. The difficulties of love will turn from the bumbling grunts of animals to the patient comprehension of a library. Love will be literature mastered by scholars alone. It is a ludicrous fantasy, but an attractive one. Epistolary love is real and does exist, but then again, they thought semaphore would surround the world in love's embrace and it didn't. Let's admit what we are talking about, and it's Hannah, of course. Of course, the body is everything.

Daemon of the library In the morning, as Raymond rides the narrow Robarts escalator to the fourth-floor reading room, he watches for a man he has come to think of as the elder, the ultimate reader, the daemon of Robarts Library. No matter how early Raymond arrives, the old man is already there.

Time has curved him like a hockey stick, and he has to use two crutches to keep his glacially slow movements somewhat steady. Distinct urine stains overlap in patches on the front of his pants. He smells. He shakes. Still, every day the old man climbs to the newspaper room on the library's fourth floor. There he scribbles letters to whatever editorial boards he happens to be angry with that day. Somnolently, disgustingly graceful, he departs when his work is done five or six hours later, and he may as well be a ghost, a stone rattling in Raymond's brain cage, a dream dreamt by someone in his place.

Seeing the fetid spectral man for the nth time, Raymond is suddenly willing to pay whatever it costs for escape if possible. Jerusalem. Raymond runs to the travel agent, who gives him a slip of paper in exchange for a grand and says, "With any luck, the troubles will have quieted down by then," with a big smile after the sale.

Shiver and shudder

Date: January 22 (5:10:58 pm)
Subject: Orchestrated apartment

Orchestrated apartment

Dear Raymond,
You have purchased the tickets! At long last! I'm overjoyed! I'm relieved! But there are a few things that you should know about the apartment situation.

I've discussed your stay with the women here and they all welcome it. We won't even have to pay extra rent. My bed is only slightly larger than a twin, and my room is small, but we won't need much physical space anyway, I'm thinking.

More important and more difficult will be all the Jewish stuff you have to remember. The kitchen is kosher, remember, so no *prosciutto e melone*. No smoking or working on Shabbat, even for you. No ripping toilet paper that day. No turning on lights. No cooking. No nothing. Can you handle it?

I'm very excited.

Love you,

H.

Date: January 23 (9:12:04 am)
Subject: re: Orchestrated apartment

Hannah,

As for the religious details, great. It will add local colour, though as I recall everyone in the apartment is in fact of American, not Jerusalemite abstraction. I will add foreign colour, then. As long as there's a bed with you in it, I'll be fine. We all have our craziness.

Love,

Ray

Date: January 24 (3:00:07 pm)
Subject: re: re: Orchestrated apartment

By the time you've been here for a week, the apartment will be a sanctuary of sanity. Jerusalem comes stocked with every variety of insanity known to man. Religious fundamentalism, nationalism and political extremism can be found within ten minutes' walk of the apartment. Ripping some toilet paper Friday afternoon won't seem so bad, trust me.

Just received the magazines! You are a doll. I must go read them. So much variety in the package, I would fall in love with you if I hadn't already.
Love,
H.

Date: January 27 (9:43:57 am)
Subject: re: re: re: Orchestrated apartment

Hannah,
I'm happy you're happy about the magazines. Looking out over the sludge/snow on St. George, I want to be reading them with you right now. I want to be reading anything but what I'm supposed to. I am meeting with my supervisor soon, which gives me something to fear, but not enough. There's not really enough even to fear.

You waste your life getting these degrees. I suppose that's obvious. Just look around a humanities department, but . . . I don't know. Books don't know how old or young you are. Spend so much time collecting that you don't read. Am I making sense? That's a rant for another message.

This year in Jerusalem! (Pretty good that I know that at least.)

Love you,

Raymond

Part 3, section 2, member 5, subsection 3

"Some are of the opinion, that to see a woman naked is able of itself to alter his affection, and it is worthy of consideration, saith Montaigne the Frenchman in his Essays, that the skillfullest masters of amorous dalliance, appoint for a remedy of venerous passions, a full survey of the body."

If one lives in Asia, one does not have an unnatural desire to move there. After eating two dozen plums, one no longer has a need to gorge on fruit. A theme runs through Burton: the cure for desire is to assume that the conditions of satisfaction are already met. Am I right about that? The seraglio is the true avenue of torment. Met at some random party. Candles in glass orbs in the dark in the garden. Our week. Other women. It would be better, the logic follows, if I had no dick. True.

Raymond considers shadows

It's cold. There's no light in the evening. My shadow as noticed as me. Jerusalem is south, so there must be more light, yes? I must ask Hannah about the plain city, not just this strange half-school of theology she attends. Because I must understand. Explore a city like a woman's body, and I've never been in Jerusalem before. Nothing to remember there.

I do remember just how empty the room was, it reverberated, and how the sun poured down into the bare apartment. Hannah's a shadow, a memory with Internet words mixed in, and I am no more to her. Hannah's insubstantial, but if there's a shadow, there's light, yes?

Occasionally, in the afternoon, the day is bright and cold, and he's done all the work his brain will allow. Then Raymond strolls north or south, east or west, wherever there's a view.

Raymond takes a short break

Need a new city. Look, there is a Vietnamese neighbourhood composed entirely of two-storey houses with the second floors rented out. Compare that to the Portuguese neighbourhood just north with its two-storey houses with the second floors rented out. Farther north, the new money lives in opulent Georgian or ultramodern places. Across Yonge, the old money lives in opulent Georgian or ultramodern places. That row of prefab homes is owned entirely by Pakistanis, and that one by Italians, and that one by Poles.

Raymond considers the neighbourhoods

It's quite easy to forget you're anywhere at all.

In Toronto

Date: February 2 (2:35:53 am)
Subject: Nightclub

Dearest, dearest Raymond,
I'm in Tel Aviv. Deb and I decided to put Talmud aside for a few days and hit the clubs for a little Hellenism. The people in these clubs, Raymond, gorgeous. We couldn't even get into the one that was recommended to us, because it opens at four in the morning, and we are just too wasted already. Dancing in a city filled with beautiful, fit soldiers is, as you would imagine, an experience. Hedonism here is really an "ism" like the rest: communism, surrealism, etc. An ideology and way of life. The proximity to death stirs the loins, that's what Deborah says. It also does something to the skin. Everyone seems to glow. Bus just arrived. Deborah screaming. Bye.
Love,
H.

If Raymond had a Daytimer, in many months of blank pages there would be only a single entry: Monday, February 3. Since he has no Daytimer, in fact no calendar other than on the bottom right-hand corner of his computer screen, the time has been inscribed in his mind since the date was set. Meeting with his supervisor at her office, 3:15 p.m.

In the colleges of the university, the temperature is either too warm or too cold, the decor either luxurious with rich wooden panelling or roughly squalid, pieced together with twine and particle board. Paint cracks off the walls above elaborate nineteenth-century carvings on the banisters and windowsills. Precious libraries filled with first editions are held up by brick and plank shelves.

Jane is on the phone when he arrives for their appointment at 3:13 exactly, but she motions him in. "Mm-hmmm . . . yes . . . yes . . . mm-hmm." She is wearing sweatpants and a cheap red and gold chinoiserie top. He sits awkwardly in a chair facing her and tries to adjust to the cold while she is locked to her phone call.

B.A. (Toronto), M.A. (Oxford), Ph.D. (Harvard). Who Jane Stocher is Nearly two decades ago, Crazy Jane wrote a passably interesting, frequently footnoted article about Thomas Browne's *Pseudodoxia Epidemica*, which Raymond once sort of admired. She's forty-seven, two years into menopause but young and edgy by the university's standards.

In the quadrangle, from which light is streaming, Professorial office the chickadees are trilling, the boughs of mature trees are weighted with snow. Inside the office are limy coffee pots, unread journals, strange outfits, fingerless gloves.

"Raymond?" Supervision

"Excuse me. Yes?" Raymond has been daydreaming out the window.

"Raymond. Sorry. Raymond. Sorry about this. Daughter just landed at Pearson. Clean forgot.

I've just got to meet her. Sorry, sorry."

"Oh. That's all right."

Crazy Jane begins gathering her belongings from the overflowing desk. "Keep reading. Keep noting. Meeting in March, you know. With the whole committee."

"Right."

"Sorry about this, but daughter's at the airport, you see."

"Of course, of course."

"Back to the books."

This couldn't have worked out better, Raymond thinks as he accompanies her out of the office. Yes, back to the libraries and the apartment and the elder readers and the dead. Raymond watches Crazy Jane dash down the hallway waving to him.

Raymond at his library desk again

Dead men and their words. No one is more vulnerable, no one can you harm less. Who will reply out of the book dust? What a weird, weird business I'm in, stalking ghosts as substantial as the concrete wall I'm brushing. Rough bubbles and touch rubble and anti-flesh troubles.

Raymond considers women's bodies

Women's hands. Their arms are smooth and awkward, hirsute, depilated, leading to the power of the shoulders, the weakness. Framing the face. Beyond description. Breasts counterpointed to armpits, roundness of belly and the flatness, the cunt, the smooth or ragged leg-strength. Feet that grab the soil and stand to walk, and run. Hannah.

My friend's great-grandfather said that at fourteen, something grabs hold of you by the prick,
and it drags you along your whole life, but if you
survive long enough, it lets go.

Raymond recalls
anecdotes about
impotence

Early in the *Republic,* Socrates meets up with an
old man and asks him what being impotent is like.
He replies that it's as if a dog had been untied
from his leg.

Date: February 8 (2:15:35 pm)
Subject: Your body

Your body

Dear Hannah,
Sitting here in the library thinking about your
body. Flashes of it return to me in the oddest
places. How many others in this bank of concrete
cubicles are overcome with memories of flesh,
I wonder.

It's the middle of a Canadian winter, I should
remember. Everyone is hidden under dense layers
of cloth. Each moment outdoors is pain. That
must have something to do with it.
I love you.
Raymond

Date: February 10 (7:23:18 pm)
Subject: re: Your body

I think it will help to travel. We have less than
three months to go, if you can believe it. I'm
already picturing how we will rent a car to explore
the country. Travel will solve everything. Think

about Jerusalem. Meanwhile, strength.

Love,

H.

Raymond considers the wasted cities

Jerusalem. Istanbul and Athens. Srebrenica and Vienna. Take me to Shanghai. Take me to Lagos. Take me to Santiago. All those cities the world served up and I wasted. Thrown my eyes away on books in their places. Love is flying overhead, from the airport where I will name the city, and the plane will take us there, Hannah.

Part 1, section 2, member 3, subsection 15

"'Tis the common tenet of the world, that learning dulls and diminisheth the spirits, and so by consequence, produceth melancholy. Two main reasons may be given of it, why students should be more subject to this malady than others. The one is, they live a sedentary, solitary life, to themselves and letters, free from bodily exercise, and those ordinary disports which other men use: and many times, if discontent and idleness concur with it, which is too frequent, they are precipitated into this gulf on a sudden: but the common cause is overmuch study."

The passage is irritating. A scholar writing to other scholars within a massive work of scholarship in order to criticize scholars. Evidence either of a deficiency in Burton's humour or of his ability to keep a straight face, both equally incredible. Either way, he's wrong: I'm always wandering the frozen streets, lost to myself but not to letters. I exercise *in perpetuum*, but my mood is melancholic without doubt, and I am not the victim of overmuch study, but of boredom and wasted opportunity and horniness. Or are these values equivalent?

Date: February 14 (8:47:09 am) A & E
Subject: A & E

Dear H,
Happy Valentine's Day. Incredible. When I think about how all this started. One week of sexual presence. No. Not just sexual presence, but actual presence, then extended absence. We were porn stars. Now we're Abelard and Eloise.

I keep taking the plane ticket out of the drawer and staring at it and then putting it back. Then I go and hold my silver Jerusalem. I can't tell if my excitement about the trip is really about Jerusalem, or about being in any city other than moodless Toronto, or if it's just seeing you again, having a chance to relive our week over the space of the month. "All of the above" is the right answer, I guess.
Love,
R.

Date: February 14 (8:56:51 pm)
Subject: re: A & E

I think we should remember that there's only two and a half months left to go. The light at the end of the tunnel is starting to really burn.
I am your valentine.
H.

Date: February 16 (8:35:00 am)
Subject: re: re: A & E

Hannah,
Only two and a half more months of time-wasting
and self-pity. The real problem here is that I'm
starting to hate the person I am while waiting for
you. Back to reading . . .
Love you,
R.

Reading week The week arrives during which students, Raymond
included, stop reading.

Parties in February The second month of the year is always depressing, drab, costumed in boredom's regalia.
Foreknowledge of this fact does not alleviate it. The
cold and the lack of light take their toll on us. Even
parties are a burden: people rushing to places they
don't particularly want to go from places they don't
particularly want to be. Raymond's among them.
He's been invited to a party, at which he will know
no one but the host, Paul.

A scene Raymond is sitting in an armchair awkwardly
positioned between a stove and a one-unit
washer-dryer. At some distance, six or seven
women are clustered around a kitchen table
whose surface is covered with empty beer bottles,
half-finished mickeys and overflowing ashtrays.
The women are speaking to each other raucously,
but Raymond is not paying attention. He hasn't

bothered to remove his jacket, and so, when he stands up to leave, he just puts the empty bottle on the floor.

Why am I walking home alone? Hannah walks to the Old City of Jerusalem and then home through strange, white, folded streets and unimaginable smells. Exciting: for a month we will eat meals spread out over hours over her floor beside the bed or on the bed, not like now, so cold my eye sockets are as hard as a jean pocket stuffed with snow. So why am I quietly heading back to my empty apartment? Love, cities and women.

Raymond considers the walk home

Date: February 24 (8:21:10 pm)
Subject: Safed

Safed

Ray,
Just back from Safed where Jenn and I had the most wretched weekend of our combined lives, organized by an ultra-Orthodox group specializing in reclaiming "lost Jews" like us. First I must sleep.
Love,
H.

Date: February 24 (2:15:35 pm)
Subject: re: Safed

Tell me everything. Leave out no detail.
Love,
R.

Date: February 25 (8:01:57 pm)
Subject: re: re: Safed

Okay. I am somewhat refreshed, after a good
night's sleep and a fruitful day's study.

Safed is a small town north of Jerusalem, filled
with the creme de la creme of religious nutbars.
Jenn and I arrived on Friday afternoon, just
before Shabbat. As we were walking down to the
hostel, six black-hatters and a horse came toward
us, like a greeting party. The men were dancing
around the horse, not touching it, as if they were
scared to, while at the same time they couldn't
stop following it, shouting at us to get out of the
way. I was completely mystified, but Jenn figured
it out right off. Somebody's horse had escaped,
but they couldn't touch it because the Sabbath
had just begun. Obviously, they couldn't just let it
run wild either. Straight out of medieval Poland,
this little vision.

Another medieval relic was waiting for us at
the hostel in the shape of Benjamin, a small, rat-
shaped man with tiny, violent eyes who had vol-
unteered to host us for dinner. Dinner was part
of the deal with this tour. The walk to his house,
after he had seen that we were settled, was his
big chance for autobiography. He had been born
into a secular family in California, found religion after his dissolute twenties, and was deep
in his studies of kabbalah. By the time we
arrived at his house, it was clear to both Jenn
and I that we were dealing essentially with a cult

member. His semi-comatose wife and six children lived in squalor.

The meal was entirely white. Boiled potatoes with a filet of sole, canned veggies, I shit you not. Then he spent the whole evening ranting about secularism, the failure of the Diaspora, the holiness of the Holy Land, and the traitorous dealings with the Palestinians under the "disguises of peace." What really shocked me though was that it was boring. It was nothing more than a nightmare suburban dinner with family you can't stand. They had no pictures on the wall, because that would be iconography, and no books other than religious books. Jenn insisted on arguing with the kabbalist about women in Judaism. Benjamin's wife was silent throughout. I can't even say if husband and wife shared a language.

The feminist versus the kabbalist was not a fight I ever expected to witness, but it did clear up which side I am on. I suppose the kabbalist never had a chance after serving us whitefish with boiled potatoes. Ugh. It was just so awful, Raymond.
Love you,
Hannah

Date: February 26 (10:35:24 am)
Subject: re: re: re: Safed

What did you do, though, after the meal?

Date: February 27 (7:23:15 pm)
Subject: re: re: re: re: Safed

Dinner came to end, we'd paid our dues, the rest of the weekend was ours. Thanks God there are some cool historic synagogues in Safed, or else the whole trip would have been a waste.

I feel like I'm having a tempestuous affair with Judaism. It's beautiful and I love it, but goddamn sometimes it pisses me off.

My narcissus plant has finally started to sprout white blossoms, and they are just gorgeous. I was happy with the little green stems, but these are like cathedrals.

Love,
Hannah

Date: February 28 (10:11:56 am)
Subject: re: re: re: re: re: Safed

Hannah,
What a story. The cults of Safed being boring. It's too bad. I thought Judaism might be the one world religion I could stomach. I am not jealous of your relationship with Judaism, by the by. Keep it as a lover, as long as you write to both of us.

Love,
Raymond

Raymond addresses the peoples of the Book

Hello, Jews, I adore your libraries, and I adore your exile, and how the two are one, and the frame of your laws is elegantly beautiful. But I hope you understand that you're reading the fantastical ravings of stone-age shepherds as if they were true. And Christians, you have mastered stone, and set up houses for Jesus inscribed with gold and Bernini statues and the rich sacrifice of your martyrs' bones. You did it all for barely written-down rumours about a nutty preacher in the desert two thousand years ago. How glorious, one wants to believe. How stupid, too. Islam, you could be justified for the calligraphy alone, or for the sound of your prayers, or for the cities you built in your name, in tolerant peace, in the richness of wisdom. Your most disturbing problems, ancient and modern, would fill too many pages to list here.

You may as well believe in fairies, all of you.

Compare Raymond to a brother from any contemplative order, and there's not much for contrast. He divides his time between ecstasies of thought in his basement cell and dusty explorations in the library. Fellow scholars pass him in silence. He dreams about women whom he resists, and masturbates furiously. The only real difference between Raymond and a monk is that, on rare occasions, Raymond goes for a walk.

Secular monk

Something about these undeveloped piles of industrial filth stuffed onto abandoned sites. They're either half-built or half-ruined. Can't tell which.

Like Hannah and I.

Raymond goes for a walk to the waterfront

Still, there is Jerusalem to come.

That week with her was like drinking bubbles, that sweet. Stories of fish in the lake. Her demands for that fortune cookie, remember? Happy Gardens. And the bed was an island. Like when you pour champagne into the flute just after it's popped, and it's half bubbles and you stick your face in the glass to suck it up. When your nose gets all sugar ruffled and stuff.

And how fucking ironic, atheist me, hedonist me, for whom little is forbidden and most is permitted, I live like a monk. I live like what? Without even platonic love.

Jerusalem, soon. My committee meeting soon. Shit.

Another scene Raymond is standing at a bar, swaying slightly, drunk. Beside him, in a red silk dress, is a (very) young and (very) beautiful Chinese woman, whom he saw once at Paul's. Nineteen years old and extraordinarily thin.

Raymond: It's rebellion with Paul. His people are all frail Auntie Mame types. It crushed his mother when he got a football scholarship.

Lara: How do you know that?

Raymond: I've known Paul since we were boys in Halifax.

Lara: My point is, how could you know? Okay. My point is maybe that it's just the build. Maybe it's just that he's a big strong guy who can play football, and not just rebellion or whatever. Why's everything about rebellion? You know what I mean?

Raymond: I can see . . .

Lara: It's like everyone under thirty isn't their own person. My name's Lara by the way (cocked smile, crooked-armed handshake).

Raymond: Raymond.

Date: March 6 (10:09:41 am)
Subject: Quick one

Dear Hannah,

This is just a quick note. I have to go meet with my committee to discuss the (non)progress on my dissertation, and I must be mentally prepared for the fibbing. I think I'll tell them that I'm just going to read all the books I can find. Start at PR 1 and go to PR 9999. That will help me prepare.

Amazing how little work I'm getting done considering I spend all day in the library. It's really quite embarrassing. I'm starting to feel a bit like the old man who lives in the periodicals room. I think of him as the daemon of Robarts. He's a little hunchbacked old man with piss stains all over the front of his pants. He's me plus sixty years. Must go. Love you,

R.

Date: March 7 (2:30:51 pm)
Subject: re: Quick one

I'm afraid I don't know who you're talking about. Who is this guy?

Some good news on this end. I've been practising reading my Hebrew, and I've decided I'm going to do an aliyah next Shabbat. That's when you read a piece of the Bible in synagogue. I haven't done that since my bat mitzvah. I've been kind of planning it since New Year's, but I didn't want to wimp out at the last minute because I didn't feel ready, so I didn't tell anyone. I think I'm ready now, though. Deborah and the whole community have had to prod me a bit, but now I'm more excited than nervous.

I'll tell you how it goes. You tell me how your meeting goes.

Love,

H.

Meeting of the committee

The office reserved for dissertation committee meetings is in the department building. The deliberate odour of mildew permeates the room.

The two other members of Raymond's committee sit on either side of Crazy Jane. They are old enough, and she has dressed wildly enough, to give the impression that they are her chaperones. Forget their names. Raymond has. His slight anxiety makes him feel pathetic more than anything: apparently he can be made nervous by them. They are culture, these professors, culture being another word for mould. Moulding him. The room is full of silence and mildew and Raymond's nerves.

Where his work is at

When they ask, he tells them that he's still taking notes, and thinking about the general direction of the book. Measure twice, cut once. The answer must be completely unacceptable, he thinks, but it's all he has.

"That's good. Quite right. End of your third year coming up, isn't that right, Raymond? Now let me tell you about when I was doing my dissertation at Harvard. I changed periods three times. At Harvard, I started out in modernism, turned about your stage of studies to Shakespeare, then decided I wanted to be with Sir Thomas. Thomas Browne, you know. So I wouldn't worry. I'm not worried.

Crazy Jane on how she wrote her thesis

"And when I got down to it, started writing it, you know, I had exactly two months. Otherwise, no job without it. Needed to write it, you see. My supervisor said—and no one believes this part of the story—my supervisor told me to put five pages a day on his desk. Every day. Five pages. And so it was written. My dissertation."

The other professors chortle at Crazy Jane's anecdote, laugh outright at the one that follows, and soon Raymond is mercifully forgotten. God bless Jane Stocher. They are telling their own tales of when they wrote their dissertations back in 1846 or something. 1966. Geriocracy. Raymond can sense, like the subtle shift of a season, the hour coming to an end. This couldn't have worked out better, he's thinking.

What does he do now? Read?

Free at last

139

Date: March 10 (11:12:31 am)
Subject: Meeting went well

Hannah,
Meeting went well, I think. We talked about their
work instead of mine. Big relief.

Only a month and a half of reading left, then
Jerusalem and you will be my lovely reward.
Love,
Raymond

"Yet what I have formerly said of other Melancholy,
I will say again, it may be cured or mitigated at
least, by some contrary passion, good counsel and
persuasion, if it be withstood in the beginning,
maturely resisted, and as those Ancients hold, the
nails of it be pared before they grow too long. No
better means to resist or repel it, than by avoiding
idleness, to be still seriously busied about some
matters of importance, to drive out those vain
fears, foolish fantasies, and irksome suspicions out
of his head, and then to be persuaded by his judi-
cious friends, to give ear to their good counsel and
advice, and wisely to consider, how much he dis-
credits himself, his friends, dishonours his children, disgraceth his family, publisheth his shame,
and as a Trumpeter of his own misery, divulgeth,
macerates, grieves himself and others; what an
argument of weakness it is, how absurd a thing in
its own nature, how ridiculous, how brutish a passion, how sottish, how odious; for as Hierome well
hath it, others hate him, and at last he hates

himself for it; how hare-brain a disease, mad and furious! If he will but hear them speak, no doubt he may be cured."

This is Burton's cure: floods of words endlessly poured upon the head of the sufferer. Drench the man in verbiage. Soak him in phrases until he can no longer remember his sickness.

When Burton mentions friends, he means books. Consequently, when he quotes books, it's as if he's mentioning friends. His friends drown his sorrows in buckets and buckets of words, but still he isn't cured, so he edits and re-edits his book, adding enough significant chunks of material for five different versions. Nothing filled up the melancholy hole in Robert Burton's soul. All the particulars of the world's misery, disease, disorder and depression couldn't fill it. The worlds of words written down in a book. Love couldn't fill it. Give me the thickness of a mane of hair, alcohol and dancing, my fist in snow, the mouth grip of peanut butter, the weight of a sauna's warm stone in my palm and a whole new city. Anything but keyboard clatter or desk wood, the flats and edges of books.

Another woman. Beautiful and vague. Not timid, but vague. Nineteen years old. Twenty? Virgin? No. Not that look about her. Chinese. With make-up. Decorated woman. Lara.

> Raymond considers Lara

And it's March. Papers and nature are due. The crocuses sprout duly at the roots of poplars and

> Raymond smells spring

pines. The rain is replacing the snow. College Street should burst flagrantly soon, and life will again be rich and fragrant. Any moment now the smell of spring will pour down like an overturned bucket. A hint. Nitrogen? Peasant mud? Pollution slushy smell, premeditating the sweetness of crocuses in gutter dust.

Raymond looks up

When he looks down College Street, Raymond wants summer to come. That's when the action in this godforsaken city is. All the women are wearing wool coats or puffy down-filled jackets now. In summer, they will pull the beautiful bodies out of storage, and he will get down on his knees and thank heaven for feminism and multiculturalism.

Raymond considers
feminism and
multiculturalism

Without feminism, there would be no girls in short skirts with bare midriffs and no intelligent women with whom to discuss the meaning of modern drama. Without feminism, there would be only wives and whores and maidens, and no glorious mixture of all three. In every city, they should name a square after Gloria Steinem, and in this square should be a statue (equestrian perhaps) of Germaine Greer. Feminism has made love, or something like it, possible.

And without multiculturalism, glory, glory, hallelujah, there wouldn't be those ultra-polished, bejewelled Italian women lounging half-naked in bar windows, nor those rafts of Greek women like shots of olive oil and fresh orange afterwards. And what about those Chinese women, like reeds, suggestively handling red peppers in the open markets? None of them. None of the tough Jamaican women smoking outside the Marxist-Leninist bookstore, as beautiful as stainless steel. Imagine the city before them. It makes you want to weep—no, more, to produce a lamentation. Summer to come. Pierre Trudeau. Yes. Back to *Anatomy*. But I will be in Jerusalem where she's reading.

Date: March 15 (9:21:55 pm)
Subject: Aliyah

Dearest Ray,
Today I read out loud from the Torah in synagogue. I am still overwhelmed.

To be honest, the moment of reading itself was more like an anxious dream than a real communion with the text. I did feel liberated, or I sensed, while I was reading, that I was in contact with the whole ocean of the dead. It was a conservative exhilaration.

Of course the moment I had finished, I began to wonder what I would do after Jerusalem. Luckily I'll have to think about it later, because I have to go now. Friends from the Institute have prepared a celebratory dinner for me.
Love you,
Hannah

"Some do not obscurely make a distinct species of it, dividing love melancholy into that, whose   Part 3, section 4, member 1, subsection 1 object is women; and into the other, whose object is God."

Of course, any particular form of melancholy can be connected to any other form. Why, here, does Burton choose to connect (by the clever means of dividing) lust and the love of God? My love for Hannah, Hannah's new love for God. We'll see in a month or so how sundered these melancholies are. What did she say so long ago about dust moving across a floor and drowned mice?

Wait, this must be about Burton sometimes and not always myself. The sundering is between himself and the world. Lust is the most direct danger to him personally, but the love of God is the most general and most crippling madness of them all, Burton is clear to state: "Give me but a little leave, and I will set before your eyes in brief a stupend, vast, infinite Ocean of incredible madness and folly: a Sea full of shelves and rocks, sands, gulfs." I can't write it, and I can't write her.

He must read more   But first he must notice—sudden warmth in the air—that spring is finally here.

Ravines   Through this anonymous city, through its commodious ugliness, its moodlessness, wild ravines run. It's as if in the rush outward to decimate the wilderness, the city incurred its own losses. Crazy wildflowers grow there, and in the spring the children run down into them to commit dangers. The adolescents follow to bushfuck and bushdrink, and the smell of the green, pocketed with snow, clears the brain of the other city dwellers. All come back up with wilderness crevices in their urban selves.

Date: March 20 (7:35:37 pm)
Subject: Call

Ray,
How rough are things getting? Your silence worries me. Perhaps you should start to see a contemporary version of the writer of *Anatomy of Melancholy*. I can recommend an excellent psychiatrist if you like. Yet another advantage to dating a Jew.

Why don't you call? Call collect. I don't care.
I love you,
H.

Date: March 21 (7:54:09 pm)
Subject: re: Call

Sorry I haven't called, it's just quasi-impossible to find a reliable time when both of us are at home. I tried the other day (okay a week ago), but I just got ringing. I panicked, thinking I'd got the time change wrong. Must go. I will keep trying to call.
Love you,
R.

"Only take this for a corollary and conclusion, as thou tenderest thine own welfare in this, and all other melancholy, thy good health of body and mind,

Part 3, section 4, member 2, subsection 6

145

observe this short precept, give not way to solitariness and idleness. Be not solitary, be not idle."

Reading requires two conditions: solitude and idleness. It takes gall to end a thousand-page book with instruction that could fit on the back of a matchbook and rule out the two conditions necessary for reading in the first place. Like ending a global encyclopedia of cookery with the advice: Best to eat potatoes only. And of course you must take the advice, because you are done reading. Your solitude and idleness are over, and you must go do something, you putz, Raymond. Talk with a Lara in a red dress at a party, say. She'll be at that bar next week, you are aware? Clean the apartment, maybe.

Cleaning the apartment

He wipes the sweaty walls, gathers the dirty clothes into a monolith, shelves the books scattered loosely on the ground, picks up his notes which are making white squalls on the floor. Owning only a Dustbuster, he must vacuum on his hands and knees, stroke by stroke. He bought a mop for the linoleum in the kitchen, though. Frigid still-winter air will help the floor dry, so he cracks open the window for the first time in months. When he returns from the laundromat, the basement is clean, bare, open and cold, and Raymond feels prepared. He just doesn't know for what.

Raymond and Hannah

When the sun rises, there will be a day that reaches out, only one. The sky will hold them. They will be an ocean apart.

There was a month in there somewhere. Not the slightest memory of it but Burton. Principally as a matter of scholarly research, Raymond, concede to take Burton's advice. And what is that? Go to the party. That lovely girl Lara will be there. Where is it again? A harbourfront bar. Jesus fuck Christ. Wear a suit jacket. Look nice. Check out the action. The action, yes. That's what your youth is for. Drink it, don't pour it in the sand.

Date: March 27 (6:14:39 pm)
Subject: Call x 2

Ray,
I think I missed you again last night. A group from the Institute took over a Yemeni restaurant and feasted. Please call me. I need to hear your voice tell me that things are still okay between us.
    Four weeks and counting.
Love you,
H.

Sleek, long zinc and frail, tall teak. Lara in that same red dress smiling from the perch of the back of a chair, oh hello, and it is an interesting opportunity, opportune moment. She looks at you, Raymond, as if you were a man. Ashtray, cigar smoke and your heart beating. Aren't you lucky? Hello again.

1) Raymond, seeing Lara at the other end of the bar, nods and waves. She smiles in return. He sidles over.

Raymond: It's been so long.

Lara: Yes. Since when?

Raymond: Since the last time, at that bar.

Lara: (feigning distraction) At the bar?

Raymond: Yes.

Lara: How are you?

Raymond: Well, I've been trying to follow a precept lately. "Be not solitary, be not idle." So far, I'm halfway there.

Lara: (shimmying her chair to one side, so that there's room) Those are excellent ideas.

He sits down beside her, and the bartender comes for his order.

2) Much later, she is leaning faintly against him, her red dress flamboyantly contrasting his black dress shirt. Their glasses are almost empty. So is the bar.

Lara: (whispering) Come home with me.

Raymond: Where?

Lara: To my apartment. Come home with me. Will you?

The luckiest guy on Yonge Street

Yonge Street starts uncertainly behind the twisted veil of the Gardiner Expressway. From the mangled touristy waterfront it struggles north, out of the weakling suburbs. Gathering force, it pushes through the industrial hinterlands, past breweries and plastics manufacturers, and by rivers beside nickel smelters and their warehouses. Then the wilderness raises its darkness. The mixed forests jut up. Smashed animal corpses litter the road, sustaining the ravens. Under its bridges flow rivers and streams too numerous to name or to remember. Yonge Street runs 1897 kilometres north and west to end in the practical anonymity of Rainy River on the Ontario–Minnesota border.

Follow it down. Follow all those set-back houses beside it, through the small towns with their coffee shops and parking lots for meeting places. Keep going through the suburbs, through the big box stores hugging the sides of the main drag, down further past the Gardiner to the water. Go right to the shore to the hotel restaurant bar, and in all that distance you won't find anyone luckier than Raymond as he gathers his coat and bag to leave with young, gorgeous Lara with the red dress on.

The walls of Lara's room are covered in promotional posters for movies and classical musicians. Looming up through the darkness, the serious eyes of Anne-Sophie Mutter shame him. The futon on which Lara is lying flat on her stomach is large enough that he can extricate himself without disturbing her. Finding his clothes is a tricky affair, since light creeps in only at the borders of thick curtains and the cracks of the door, but he manages. In the dark, he scrawls his name and his phone number. Cool, brilliant action.

Raymond wakes up elsewhere

Harsh fluorescents burn when the door opens, and when it closes Raymond can hear the woman, Lara, shifting under the bedclothes on the other side. He departs as quickly as he can, before they have a chance to talk it over.

Heaviness Having been roused, Lara goes to the kitchen table and takes an overripe banana from the bowl on the counter. She peels off its brown-spotted skin. The flat weight of flavour falls on her jaw. Raymond is out in the middle of the night, weighing the merits of what's open: after-hours clubs, twenty-four-hour coffee shops, diners dispensing slices of boxed apple pie.

Betrayal This was in a time when cables pulsed messages in light. There were phones you could hold in your pocket, radios on two frequencies, television stations broadcasting twenty-four hours a day from satellites. If you happened to be awake at 2 a.m. on Saturday, walking in a residential neighbourhood, and there was not the slightest breeze and nothing could be more peaceful, the space at that moment was a million ways freaky with invisible communication.

I'll call Date: March 30 (4:09:38 pm)
Subject: I'll call

Dear Hannah,
I'm going to be up late tonight, so I'll call around one in the morning my time. I think you should be home around then either way. If you plan to go out this evening, please write me back.
I love you,
Raymond

Long, crucifying pause. "I guess what I should know is if you're still coming to Jerusalem," Hannah says.

After Raymond tells Hannah almost everything

"I want to come. It's been on my mind . . ."

There is another long gap, at $1.69 per minute. That's more than two cents a second.

"It's good to hear your voice, Hannah."

"I'm going to have to think about this. I can't talk about this. I can't talk about it right now."

"Goodbye," he says into a dial tone.

Raymond almost reaches for a pen and paper, but decides that he can remember, on his own, which parts of his story are straight and which crooked. He has played it smart: there are only two lies to remember. He failed to mention that Lara is nineteen, and that he's seeing her again tonight.

Crooked

So she will not weep in the paper-walled apartment, or in the streets alone, Hannah goes to a Holocaust film, where her cries will be lost in the larger, more general, lamentation.

Night and Rain

Still want Hannah. Stupidest thought I've ever had.

Raymond considers folly

1) Lara is nude on the bed. Raymond is sitting at a desk flipping through piles of his notes at random, the way a bored subway rider reads a newspaper. He also is naked. Lara is tuning her violin. She does this very carefully, with an abstracted concentration that is lovely out of all measure. When this is complete:

Three scenes

Lara: Ready? (Raymond turns around. Lara sits up straight in bed. She lifts the bow to play.)

2) They are eating falafel at a park bench, but it is still cold enough to see their breath.

Raymond: Weird, I guess you could call it. I'm sleeping with you, a woman. You've just left high school. You're not even old enough to be one of my friends' students. I'd say it's weird. Wouldn't you say that's weird?

Lara: Not fair.

Raymond: (Shrugs) It's not fair, no. (Pause.)

Lara: You seem safe and real to me.

(An extended pause while they eat.)

Raymond: When do you go?

Lara: End of April. But I'm going to be really busy.

Raymond: I'm busy too.

3) Raymond and Lara are walking through the antique market on Queen's Quay. They pass shops selling family silver and jewellery and furniture and all sorts of old crap. At a stand selling prints, Raymond leans with his back to the rows of them while Lara takes them out one by one to show him. He rejects each with a shake of his head and a grimace. After nine rounds of passed images, Lara stops and they walk on.

Raymond does the math Well, our one week together was seven months ago. I was bored and alone and tired and hungry and horny and those do add up. And also, her increasing religiosity, and Lara being there, the chance of it. And I was sick of reading *Melancholy* in old, isolated Toronto. Yes, when they're all messed up, mixed together, they begin to look like a motivation. And also I'm a prick, that's another reason.

Go over it again. Raymond is far away. Raymond is not Jewish, and to break up is so obvious and so easy. So natural. Yet.

Do I just want him in my bed? Love? A week together? Toronto and Jerusalem? Let him come. Let another time decide.

Go over it again. Raymond is far away.

Hannah on complexity

When we face the reality of it, seven months ago we spent one week together and, astonishingly, neither of us has been fucking anybody else in the meantime.

Raymond begins a thought

But having come up hard on the hard fact, the pain is real.

Hannah completes it

Hannah watered her narcissi regularly. Out came light green shoots, and she continued to water. Darker stems reached straight up. Bone-white roots spread into the soil. Growing like deceit from the sweet narcissus bulbs, water + soil + information exploded in unlikely white cathedrals in the air. Now there's only the empty bowl on the kitchen table. Hannah sits staring at it, thinking about what men do.

Hannah looks at an empty bowl

Wandering-eyed, hand-roaming, some glisten in rude health; the others are prudes and cowards, disinterested. Those with appetites (without them they are nothing) can't be true, and those who do not cheat don't have the necessary appetites. Get it? Men are as innocent as this bulb, or is it innocence? Muscle tight under the skin, under the clothes.

Raymond and Lara meet every couple of days. She calls him, and he chooses a spot to meet, orderly and banal, as if no other arrangement were possible.

1) Raymond and Lara are naked on her futon. Lara is sitting up, playing the allegro movement from Bach's unaccompanied sonata number two. Raymond is listening from the pillow of Lara's right thigh, and deeply moved. When the piece ends, he applauds weakly and kisses her belly button.

2) They are at a bar (bourbon for him, beer for her). There's a long pause before they speak.
Raymond: It makes me wonder if it's me. If it's something about me.
Lara: What?
Raymond: That I seem to be with women who are about to go back to the homeland. I've been thinking about it. Before you was a Jewish girl going to Israel. You're going to China. Where are you going in China again?

Lara: Beijing first. Then they'll send me wherever.

Raymond: Right.

(Pause)

Raymond: Do you see anything in me that attracts assimilated women who want to rediscover their roots? What is it that makes me attractive to that particular sociological type?

(Pause)

Lara: I don't know. Why are you attracted to it?

Raymond: I don't know.

Lara: 'Cause I'm in it, you see. And I'm not in it, too.

Raymond: I see.

(Pause)

Lara: Do you think I should bring my violin to China? I'm kind of stressing about it.

Raymond: It's not illegal.

Lara: I figure if I stay in Beijing or any big city, it would be fine, but if I'm sent out into the country . . . If I don't practise, I'll lose it. Maybe I should buy a backup. Do you want to meet my parents?

Raymond: I do not want to meet your parents.

Lara: I was just wondering. That's fine.

(Pause)

3) Lara is on her stomach, lying flat except for the arch of her back, which Raymond is fixed on. He is not thrusting, so much as flexing and relaxing with extreme caution and focus. Lara's face is turned sideways, her eyes shifted up to stare mistily at his.

4) They are in a bad French restaurant, eating tough steak and limp frites. Raymond lifts his wine to drink and starts to speak, then stops.

Lara: What?

Raymond: It's nothing.

Lara: What were you going to ask?

Raymond: I was going to ask what universities you had applied to, but then that discussion would be too strange.

Now Lara starts to speak, and stops, but Raymond's head is down over his food, and he doesn't ask what she was going to say.

Cake Date: April 11 (11:44:19 am)
Subject: Cake

Dear Raymond,

I must tell you the truth, since you had the guts to tell me that you were having an affair, and I do believe that's no small thing for whatever pathetic little record it is. I still want to see you. However, I have been thinking about this, hard. We are over. That fact saddens me so much, Raymond, that I have tried every possible way to stop it from being true. It's still true.

Having come to an abrupt end of the attempt, I can see how crazy it was even to try. As for your trip, the hostels and hotels book up fast and I think now it will be impossible for you to find a room. So you can have your cake and eat it too. You can still stay in the apartment. We will have to do something about the rent, but I don't have the mind right now to make any decisions about that. I'm pretty much decided out at the moment.

You should probably call to make arrangements. Best regards,
Hannah

In the wake of your relief, quickly acknowledge the weirdness of the fact that you are still going to Jerusalem to stay with Hannah, acknowledge and accept that she has asked you. However. Do ensure that you have enough money to sleep elsewhere when she kicks you out. Arrive and apologize. Let her decide. Give it over. But have enough money to leave. And about Lara?

Raymond thinks strategy

Must be a pussy. Think of all those businessmen sucked off daily by their secretaries. Do they blubber and moan? No. They have wives, mistresses, no truth and reconciliation commission. Everyone knows the score. Not you, Raymond. Can't shut your mouth. You must decide, and quickly, whether you are a good man or not. Either is fine. Just stop going so limply between one and the other.

Raymond considers how men live

Under the faucet, Raymond's suspicions are confirmed: the condom has torn. His burst of panic flows into and doubles inside Lara. It becomes obvious in that moment how little they know about each other. He could be sleeping with whores for all she knows. She could be opposed to abortion. Fortunately, they're both sensible people. Morning-after-pill people.

Morning-after pill

Lara's clinic is close by. It's Saturday, the first true spring day, a middling eighteen degrees with melted marshmallow clouds, bringing out rollerbladers and women in short skirts with lapdogs in their purses and buff, shirtless men. Raymond and Lara are momentarily arrested by the enormous light, the glare of returning life. They don't want to stay outside, though. He is overcome with the desire to flee and she wants to hide.

At the clinic, there is no problem getting the appropriate chemical.

Back in her apartment, Raymond follows Lara from room to room. He won't admit the fact, even to himself, but he must watch her take it. He must see her ingest the pill. And when she does swallow it, cocking her head under the tap in the kitchen, a pitcher of relief is poured on him, spreading coolly from the top of his head to the extremities of his limbs. That's over, he thinks, that terrible door has been closed and locked forever.

The guilty thought strikes him: soon she will probably feel ill.

From outside, the jingle of a passing ice cream truck and children running after it.

When Lara cries in his arms for comfort, Raymond knows he is a substitute, but he doesn't know for whom or what.

Date: April 17 (11:45:45 am)
Subject: Flight info

Flight info

Dear Hannah,
My flight arrives at 10:13 a.m., Sunday, the twenty-fifth of April. I have your address. If need be, I can find my way to your apartment alone. I have been unable to get the same return flight as yours. Mine is three days later.
I can't wait to see you.
Raymond

His tickets are in the front drawer of his desk. They don't vanish or strike him. They don't even whimper.

The tickets to Jerusalem

1) Raymond and Lara are eating at a table covered with chapatis, chicken vindaloo, goat curry, yogurt with cucumber, nan and samosas.

Two last scenes

Lara: But you think it. How could you not think it? I see it in your face every minute we're together. I'm just a high-school girl anyway. You never listen to what I say. You would find it too embarrassing if you did.

Raymond: What does this have to do with what we were talking about?

Lara: It's got everything to do with it. Everything.

Raymond: I've never heard you talk like this.

Self-consciously dramatic to the point of ironic detachment, Lara throws her napkin on her seat and strides furiously to the bathroom.

2) She is sitting on the edge of her bed, where Raymond is lying. They are both naked.

Lara: Do you ever think about how many apples you're going to eat in your life? Three thousand, maybe? And there's going to be a last apple.

She grips him like a child and begins to cry in earnest. Raymond rubs her tensed back, and stares intently into the eyes of Anne-Sophie Mutter.

Passover

It's Hannah's best Passover ever, a true symposium rather than a bland family affair. The wide-ranging discussion of the past and freedom lingers past two o'clock in the morning, but she doesn't share a word of it with Raymond.

Raymond considers himself in a silver Jerusalem

Ruined things at the last moment, didn't you? Craving for action. Melancholic fulfillment. When you drink champagne in the darkness, it doesn't taste the same. Four days until I'm in this little city in my hand, which I have thought about in endless variations. I will be hard and silver and pure and without fear. Give it over and expect it to end.

Champagne and darkness

Raymond bought Lara a scratchy but playable fiddle from a pawnshop where it hung in a window among the other treasures that could be lived without. Violin would be too grand a word, but she can make out the allegro of Bach's second sonata, and if it gets stolen in China she won't mind too much.

Lara marked their farewell with champagne. Or sweet Spanish equivalent, anyhow. They drink silently, in the knowledge that the affair was a waste of time. They knew nothing about each other, couldn't be bothered to learn, and waited for darkness to come.

Then Raymond and Lara woke, and disentangled from each other, and went into the kitchen, and took coffee together.

Lara returned to the house of her family, before her travels to China, and saw him no more.

And Raymond remained in Toronto for three days.

When three days had passed, and all that he possessed had been placed in storage, he returned to the airport, and showed his ticket, and entered the waiting area for the flight to Tel Aviv. The flight was delayed, so Raymond sat in the airport bar and drank Manhattans. This was his twenty-sixth birthday, and neither woman knew the date.

Then the flight lifted from the ground, flew over the North Atlantic, over Europe, and into the city of Tel Aviv.

Raymond roused himself, and brushed the dust of travel off, and he was in the country of Israel then.

The security men checked his papers, and let him into the light of day.

And Hannah was waiting for him at the gate, and they embraced and looked into each other. And she said, "You are here." And he said, "Here I am."

And a taxi took them to Jerusalem, and dropped them at the house where Hannah lived. Raymond and Hannah went to the room that belonged to her, and Raymond undid his baggage: he put his garments into her closet. He put his towel among her towels. He laid his toothbrush beside hers.

They spoke of this and that, of Toronto and Jerusalem, of their past and the little future.

And when Hannah's foot grazed his, by accident, as they were outstretched, Raymond jumped, shocked.

Their touch when they touched was like cloth and static.

Their clothes they left in a pile beside the bed, and they embraced on that bed.

And after embracing, Hannah rose and dressed and went to the kitchen. She returned to where Raymond lay naked, and brought into the bedroom a plate of hummus, and eggplants stewed in oil, and there was pita and vegetables of all kinds good to eat.

As Raymond ate them, Hannah wept.

When she left the room, Raymond slumbered. And he woke at three in the morning, and Hannah was curled at his side, and he went back to sleep.

When Raymond woke for the second time, Hannah was not by his side. The sun was high. The floor of Hannah's room was flooded. On all sides of him, on the surface of the tiles, pooled a solid finger-width of water.

And he looked through the other rooms of the apartment, and they too were flooded. Though he knocked on all the doors, there was no other person in the apartment.

So Raymond searched for the cause, and found it: the washing machine poured off into the bathtub, and the drainage tube had disconnected. Therefore, the fluid had wasted itself on the floor.

And he travelled Jerusalem in search of a mop, and discovered that there are no mops in Israel, but only thick, folded cloths to wipe floors, of which he purchased twenty.

And Raymond returned to the empty apartment, and set to work on it, and after four hours the apartment was clean and dry. And he slept.

Deborah's commentary

Deborah is carefully examining the smoke rising from her cigarette when the jangle of Hannah putting her keys on the dresser smashes the reverie. "He's still asleep," Deborah says. "I think the washing machine disconnected again. The whole apartment is clean, anyway, and he must have done it somehow since the towels are still dry."

"Wow."

"Welcome to the place, could you clean it? Nice introduction." She flicks her hair back to have a straight look at her red-eyed friend.

"He's asleep?" Hannah asks.

"I think so. Good-looking guy."

Deborah must have heard them last night, Hannah thinks, creeping into the bedroom as her friend stubs out her cigarette and glances away.

A Canadian in Israel. What are you doing here?
Like meeting a Jew in rural Ontario. Maybe that's
why we're apparently fucking. Shit, I hope
Deborah didn't hear us. Not my lover, my countryman. Oh no. No no no.

He sleeps tensely, like a dog.

I was meagre when he met me. I was thinner.
My body has ripened, shall we say. All that chal-
lah and rugelach and boreka. He looks withered.
Still, you just slept with him, Hannah dearest.
The moment you saw each other, naked you fell
to the floor, and what the hell does that mean?
Countryman?

Here I am. Newness, strangeness, the room
smells like cigarettes, she must be used to it. Back
to sleep. With Hannah, this is same old, same old.
Powerful swaths of light. Memories of another
woman, too. Buying prints in the Queen's Quay
market, why would that be the one to carry across
the ocean? Then Hannah's eviscerating body. First
and last week, they are both the shocking same.
Back to sleep.

When Raymond wakes again, it's the Sabbath, and
he hears for the first time the sound of a city possessed by the dead. And Raymond is clueless:
there is no precedent and no legislation regarding
their situation. Clarity arrives in waves of jet lag
dissolving, but he doesn't want it: the problems
are too obvious and fierce. He is not a Jew and
Lara's spectre haunts his body and Hannah is

aware. Not even the cool certainty of rage satisfies her. He keeps his mouth shut.

The next morning, suspended, she leads him from the German Colony to the Old City. The usual tourist amusements and endless bundles of forgettable souvenirs are sold under the remnants of Israelite or Roman or Saracen influences. Wreckage on wreckage on wreckage.

Hannah's city

"Do you go to the Wall quite a bit, then?" Raymond asks with overcompensating politeness.

Conversation with banana ice cream outside David's Tower

"Almost never." Because they can't engage the obvious impossibility of the situation, they'll talk about tourism.

"Really."

"It's like anything." Nodding her head in the direction of an IDF soldier with a machine gun. "I went down to the Wall lots the first two weeks, but once you've seen it . . ." Hannah shrugs.

"People adapt to anything."

Hannah considers this for a few licks. "That's true." She stares at the soldier, pausing.

"What?"

"Nothing. It's that you still always know it's there. You stop thinking it's weird that every time you want to buy fruit you pass security. You stop noticing the guns. You forget about the Wall, the Dome, all the churches, but you're still in Jerusalem. It's there. You're in it."

165

The man under the Roman arch

An old man sitting on the stairs at the gate of David's Tower is a perfect point of reference for a passing tour guide. He is resting from carrying two heavy baskets of fruit and vegetables. The guide and the tourists are interested only in the Roman arch above his head. And he pays them no mind, continuing to scribble a grocery list or something on his lap.

Raymond on froth

Say nothing because you know nothing. Hannah leads me through these mazes, though I wish it were by hand. Last night's depth plumbed was not a celebration. Light as grease froth, frothy as wave scum.

Hannah on Raymond in the Old City

This man beside me simply cannot know where he stands, where he walks, what he smells, the tastes, the calls, the web of messages said but not spoken. Buy him a map then.

Conversation in the souk

Just outside the dense shadows of the covered walkways, the men in booths hawk American cigarettes and phone cards, and the melon sellers are so confident that they offer free slices to anyone who asks. After a bite, no customer refuses. She says, "You'll have to meet my roommates soon."

"You explained what happened."

"It had happened before. That washing machine's from before the Yom Kippur War."

"I worry."

"You shouldn't. About that." Then she pulls him to the edge of the pavement just before a boy races a huge cart down the narrow passage.

On the Via Dolorosa, where every few yards is marked out in stations, she buys him a fold-out map, and circles the location of the apartment with a red pen. As they approach Damascus Gate, she traces their route with a delicate, carefully filed fingernail.

Via Dolorosa

"I leave you," Hannah says, lighting a cigarette.

Conversation at the Damascus Gate

"You're leaving? You're smoking?"

"Yeah. I still need to study." He looks forlorn. "What's wrong?" she asks.

"I thought today you were going to show me the Old City. And I didn't know you smoked."

"I have to study. I have to. I have one more week in this community that is vitally important to me, and I'm not going to be in the same city with any of these people again. After this week, fuck it, we'll go on a trip or something."

He calls after her. He calls her name twice, but she doesn't turn back, and maybe the sound was lost in the melon sellers' shouts or the dust, but Hannah's hips are sweetly weaker, her walk is smoother than it's been in eight months, and Raymond picks up her scent on his hands. That is no answer.

And since (fuck him) I've seen the Old City over and over and he (fuck him) hasn't over and over,

She goes

he can go through those mazes alone. Let him stay (fuck him) and there's his answer. Lara.

He stays She smokes. She goes. I shouldn't be surprised. We only knew each other for a week. Give it up. Do the math. Resignation and I'm alone. Back into the unsweaty shade of the covered walkway.

Talking with Jenn "It's not because . . . ?" Jenn ends her question with a quizzical expression, ready to be appalled. If Hannah were ending the affair because Raymond isn't Jewish, it would be an insult to her, a betrayal of their unified front.

"No," Hannah says. She doesn't add that this fact doesn't help either.

Jenn seriously considers. "If you want my honest opinion, the straight stuff, then dump away. You must dump him. No couple ever recovers from an affair. Muscular trust, the kind that's in your bones, you know, that's comforting in a man, once that's broke, it's broke. Fixes are myths."

Talking with Deborah Hannah begins crying confused, inevitable, startled tears, so Deborah takes her into the bathroom, the only place in the apartment where privacy is guaranteed. "Hannah, listen to me. Admit at least you still have feelings for this guy, and . . ."

"I don't."

"You don't? You slept with him."

"Biology."

168

Deborah knows better than that. "I'll tell you what. People are leaving, nobody knows where ... Breathe."

"I am breathing, and I can't believe you're leaving."

Deborah lights a cigarette and hands it to her friend. "Go on. Breathe." Hannah breathes and sobs and breathes and takes one deep breath, and another. Then she takes the cigarette from her friend's fingers.

The women who share the apartment with Hannah are only too happy to have another member in the household, they say, welcoming Raymond to Jerusalem. Still, despite the outward signs of approval, Raymond perceives an awkwardness, a vagueness about the gestures of greeting. He can't for the life of him place it. After the final introduction, he realizes that what he senses is disapproval. It's prejudice. Being white, gentile and Anglo-Saxon, Raymond is completely unfamiliar with this condition. He has read about it, of course. The Jewesses disapprove of a man of his ethnicity sleeping with a Jewess. Their disapproval is fuelled not by hatred, that he can see, but by a self-conscious communal anxiety.

Or is it just that he is a cheater, a contemptible womanizer?

And that vagueness in Hannah's eyes must be embarrassment. It is embarrassment in her soft eyes. She's embarrassed to be with a goy. A whole new problem rises to crowd out the ones he can't solve. He goes for a walk alone.

Raymond considers Lara's body while lost in East Jerusalem

Garbage. Children playing in it. Lara tightening her fiddle strings, her belly flexing to sit up, the pillows of hip fat widening. Everyone on this street knows just how lost I am. Flash of the Holy Dome. Okay. I am lost but headed in the right direction. Back to the Occident. Crouched over me, Lara, as if to protect a precious thing as big as herself. That piece by Bach. The children are playing soccer with a ball of duct tape. Looks like fun, callused bare feet on all of them. This is Jerusalem. East side, west side. No end in sight.

Rabbi Katz in conclusion

"Let me repeat myself. Let me repeat myself in a different way. You recall the custom regarding coming to the end of Torah or Talmud. No matter how late the study goes, no matter how tired everyone is, we cannot finish our session at the end of a given text. We are enjoined to recommence before concluding. This is most important. Pay attention. At the end of the book, go on to the next book. If at the end of the last book, go back and start the first. Never finish. This is our custom.

"And so, there is happiness mingled with pain. There will never be any conclusion, there are only closing remarks. No matter what you have learned over the past year, and we all hope that we have helped you to live more Jewishly, no matter what you have learned, it is only the beginning. It should only be a beginning. It can only be a beginning. There is plenty more work to be done.

"But there is a joyful compensation as well. For us, there is no parting. There is only taking leave."

When we said goodbye, in Jack's sentimental Jewish eyes I could see my grandfather the last time, sick, a week and a half before he died. Jack looked just like the grandfather who gave the money for this trip and so much wanted me to marry a Jewish guy. That was my grandfather's idea. What's my idea?

Hannah takes leave from Rabbi Katz

Bright, having Ray come here. Now there's a goodbye dinner, goodbye to all my Judaism friends, here's the goy I'm shtupping. My idea. Hello, goy, here's all my Judaism. Bright, bright, bright, Hannah, one after another.

Hannah considers her bright ideas

"I'm regretting this dinner already. The problems? Oy." Deborah chooses a light blue shirt from the closet and begins dressing.

Deborah's view of the matter

"The community needs a chance to say goodbye," Hannah says, distantly. She is flipping through a year-old *People* magazine on Deborah's bed.

"Sure, but I wish we had invited only the people we like. Josh is coming to this thing, you realize."

"I realize."

Deborah finishes buttoning her shirt. "Hannah? Don't worry about Raymond. No one will have a problem."

"No?"

"What do you give a shit about them for, anyway? After tonight, you'll never see them again. Hannah?"

Hannah does not look up from the best-and-worst-dressed photo spread, which she's already read a dozen times.

Raymond addresses himself on himself

Now let us turn our attention, Raymond, to the question of Raymond. Here is an interesting case indeed, for we have the WASP pluralist brought into contact with otherness, brought into a world that does not share his values, in which it is not his prerogative, because he is powerless in the matter, to bring about the conditions of a "common ground." Let us see how he responds.

Final Shabbat dinner

Eight months together at the Institute and now, after a last meal, they'll disband to cities across North America to see how long they can stay good Jews. The meal has been prepared by the women of the house: grilled eggplant and zucchini, couscous with raisins, and a yogurty soup. The guests have brought bread and wine.

Raymond is of little interest, though he does add a wistful touch to the evening, a quiet reminder of their imminent return to exile. At the washing of the hands and the blessings, his self-exemption renews the almost forgotten knowledge that for most people these rituals are foreign. Then Joshua notices that this last supper is like its predecessor in that there are thirteen Jews at the table—but he forgot about Raymond, of course. There are only twelve Jews, plus Raymond, who doesn't hesitate to single himself out jokingly as Judas or Christ, they can take their pick. Everyone laughs, but Hannah's laugh is nervous.

Raymond sits terribly still, like a man in a hospital during the surgery of a loved one. Hannah is distant, distracted more than engaged by the shifting conversational tides. A renewed argument over whether Judaism is compatible with feminism finds both men and women taking the position that women are too holy to need scheduled prayer, and are set aside out of preference to the importance of the home. There's a man who talks about his dream of working in the YIVO Yiddish library in New York. Pamela discusses her plans to join a settlement outside Bethlehem. Hannah listens carefully, nervously: thanks God nobody asks about her plans. They talk Israeli politics: what the Arabs are thinking, what Barak is thinking, what Netanyahu; they are fierce, but it's their last Shabbat dinner, and arguments are ended with shrugs and smiles and the liberal application of the saying "Put two Israelis in the room and you have three opinions," as if they are Israelis.

The meal ends, and Raymond rises to clear the dishes, as he has been trained to do after women cook him a meal. The Canadian gesture to feminist practice startles the men in the room. The least ridiculous thing for Raymond to do is to press on, so he does. When he returns for more dishes, the party is dispersing to the living room and the patio. No Hannah in the room to observe her reaction.

The last man at the table hands Raymond his plate with what amounts to a sneer. His name is Joshua or something. It begins with a "J" anyway. "How are you liking Jerusalem?"

"Fascinating."

"You've been here how long?"

"A week."

Joshua sneers again, throwing his napkin on his plate.

The meal agreed with them. They sit talking about early Yiddish writers, the king of Jordan and the value of the shekel. Raymond's sole conversational excursion is a mention of A.M. Klein, Canadian poet and novelist, and answering a bored question about his writings. Then he retires tactfully to bed. He goes first, it is true, but everyone else leaves soon after. With open tears and hopeful, loving declarations of permanent friendship, the party dissolves, until there are only the women of the house, wiping their cheeks and doing dishes.

Raymond considers a myth as it dies That the Ivy League schools make you smarter, I think I believed before tonight, before I sat down to dinner with a roomful of people from Harvard and Yale. That the Ivy League makes you better, I even believed. Travel as a method of learning contempt for the world's peoples.

By resistance (Maccabean revolts, War of 1812) they survived the spread of conquest (Hellenism, Christianity, manifest destiny) by taking from and defining themselves against the dominant power (Rome, America).

How being Canadian is like being a Jew

"Are you asleep?" Hannah asks quietly.

"Sort of asleep," Raymond mumbles. She instantly undresses, allowing her top and skirt to fall at her feet in one swift dispersion. "They all seemed very nice."

"We'll talk in the morning." Click of earrings out of ears, necklace unclasped.

"It was nice." Bra unhinged joins the other clothes on the floor.

"We'll talk in the morning."

Her cool nakedness surrounds his hot back, and they doze in each other's arms as if there were no history.

Conversation after Hannah creeps into the bedroom

Those are my people, and as they disband, I disband. I have no idea what to do in Toronto. No idea who to be. Oh, Deborah, how can you go? Tomorrow? Tomorrow, your room will be bare, I'll walk into it, and it will depress me, lower me to the ground. Those are my people, no matter whose warm, lovely body I'm wrapped around.

Hannah considers the ebb of the future

Raymond and Hannah are still fucking. Again and again and again.

One thing that should be made perfectly clear

In the morning, when Hannah emerges, Deborah is sitting on her suitcase in the hallway, lighting a cigarette. When she does notice Hannah, her smile beams, her eyes brim.

"I was going to wake you. The cab's here any minute."

Hannah helps her take the suitcase down to the curb, and waits with her until the taxi comes. "I'm leaving just as the story gets good. There's e-mail, thank God, so use it. Now here's my cab. I love you."

"I love you too, Deborah."

"What's Toronto–New York, an hour by plane? We'll be fine."

"I don't know who I'm going to talk to."

"Me. That's who you're going to talk to. E-mail." Together they load the back of the cab with luggage. "Hannah, shalom."

For a second, Hannah feels that the word means peace. To Deborah, she says, "Shalom."

Hannah pulls down the wool blanket covering the glass of the French doors. There's no need for it any more. Deborah's room is empty except for a few curled papers in the corner, crumbs, bits of fallen plaster. The room itself looks like an absent friend.

It is the Sabbath again, so once again Jerusalem is suspended. The gravity of prayer is the only weight that could keep it from floating into the air. Raymond and Hannah eat figs together and their bodies still look for each other, in silence, with neither yes nor no.

Abraham loved Sarah, and Sarah bore him Isaac. Abraham loved Isaac, and he loved God. He journeyed to a hill three days from his home, and lifted his sword to kill Isaac, but did not. Instead, he found a ram and sacrificed it on the hill. That hill was Jerusalem.

David loved Saul, and he loved him out of Jerusalem; and he loved the Philistines, and he loved them to the sea. The Israelites loved themselves, until the Assyrians loved them, and the Israelites had to love them back. The Babylonians loved the Israelites out of Jerusalem, and their lovemaking left Jerusalem in ruins, but it was rebuilt. The city is always rebuilt. The Persians loved the Israelites into Jews. And the Greeks loved the Persians, loved them to submission. The Greeks loved themselves. The Syrians loved the Greeks. The Syrians loved the Jews. The Jews loved the Syrians so hard that they became Israelites again and ruled over Jerusalem.

The Romans loved the Israelites who loved the Romans, and the Romans loved the Israelites until Jerusalem was burning, and until the Israelites were again Jews. The Romans loved themselves into Byzantines. The Persians loved the Byzantines and the Byzantines loved them back, until the Muslims came, and there was no love in Jerusalem.

The Christians, however, were full of love. They adored the Muslims and the Jews, and the

Muslims adored the Christians, until they forced them out. The Turks loved the Ayyubids. The Mamelukes loved the Turks. The Ottomans loved the Mamelukes. The British loved the Ottomans. They loved the Jews and the Arabs, and the Jews and the Arabs loved them back until they departed. The Jews loved the Arabs, and the Arabs loved the Jews, and they loved each other into Israelis and Palestinians, and they are loving each other still, mixing their dust together in Jerusalem, opening their bodies to each other in Jerusalem.

Love in Jerusalem in May That May saw no bulldozings of homes, no blowing up of schoolbuses, no settlers' outrage other than the location of their existence. In a foreign country, in a language neither side spoke, the suspended fate of the city was being negotiated, before it all dissolved in fear and contempt.

Raymond and Hannah in love In silence, in bed, they are incapable of discussing or measuring or convincing. Dumb bodies that need to speak, they hide from themselves in each other. Healing and wasting, their naked selves falling apart and decaying, their bodies continue. Their bruises colour and fade. Confusion flourishes in the river that doesn't flow through the city, and their bodies ripen, rot, and close in on the end of a month in Jerusalem.

Raid to Elat Jerusalem is the reason they're not talking, they decide. A three-hour bus ride across the Negev takes them all the way to the Red Sea, to a pleasure town called Elat that has a ritzy promenade by the beach. That's where they will be able to talk. Sure enough, after they've settled in a hostel and strolled out beside the sea, conversation comes to them like a breeze. The faint sounds of a jazz singer doing "A Sailboat in the Moonlight and You" drift from a café filled with soldiers on leave.

"It's over," she begins.

A sailboat in the moonlight and you

He looks down at his feet. "Is it over?"

"We had a week. The week ended. We tried to keep it together because it was so wonderful and because e-mail was fun. You started seeing another woman. How can it not be over?"

He considers mentioning the intercourse of that very morning, but there is no need. The memory is as present to them as the boats clanking offshore in the darkness.

"It's good to talk with you, at least, at last," he says.

"I came here for you," he says.

Wouldn't that be heaven

"That was the wrong reason, then. You should have come for Jerusalem."

"I didn't come for Jerusalem. Please listen to me."

"What?"

He stares out at the sea. He can see the lights of both Egypt and Jordan from the beach.

"What is it?" Hannah repeats.

"I should listen to you," he replies.

Tears are relieving. They leave the promenade and jump over the waist-high edge of its border to sit behind the cover of a rock on the sand, in the darkness beside the sea, and sob. Raymond offers his arm for comfort, and Hannah accepts without reluctance. The frustration ebbs but as it sloshes and waves off, the base facts remain. He is not a Jew, and Lara's presence will not evaporate. But they try. They throw themselves against the insolubility of their lives again.

"The situation was my fault. I don't want to pretend that that's untrue. But what I'm saying. This is what I'm saying . . . We're in this situation. The situation's my fault, I know. I don't want to excuse myself, or say, 'Let's pretend it never happened,' but this is the situation. And we should do what's best." Simple, practical man speaking. That's the spirit.

"And you think that is?"

"I think we should be together."

Only the faintest light illuminates the angles of her face as it drifts away from him and then flashes back. "I refuse to let you say, 'It's my fault,' to let you take the blame for this. To let you say, 'It's my fault,' and then make me forgive you, or not. Put it on me. The relationship came to an end and then . . ."

"Then what?"

"Then it was over."

"I don't know what to say to that," he replies.

"Why did you come? Why did you fucking come here?"

They help each other to stand, and brush off their jeans, leap over the half-wall to the promenade, Hannah first.

A chance to drift for you to lift

"It is serious," Hannah says.

"But why does it always have to be serious? Why can't it be: we have fun? It is fun."

"This is fun, this talking?"

They have arrived at the point where the promenade opens into a fairgrounds, identical to North American versions down to the whack-a-mole. A Ferris wheel floods it in light.

"This playground is my idea of fun. Let's leave all this bullshit talk, all this serious conversation, and go on some rides."

Hannah stares blankly at the fair. It does look like fun.

Your tender lips to mine

They walk back the way they came. The sounds of the jazz singer reappear, under Raymond's voice. "We just can't be beaten by timing. We can't let bad timing ruin . . ."

"What's that?"

"We can't let timing dictate to us. We should refuse that."

She stretches her arms down into her pockets. "You can't refuse history. That's nobody's choice."

The things dear

That I long for "Because you are simply not a Jew," Hannah says.

"That's disgusting."

"It's true."

"It's not fucking true."

She is embarrassed by the vehemence of his response, answering in hushed intensity. "I didn't invent the history of the Jewish people, and I would have done it differently myself, but it happened. It's happening. And please keep your voice down. Everyone here speaks English."

He repeats flatly, "That's disgusting."

Are few The Israeli soldiers are lounging against the back speakers on the temporary stage where the jazz singer sings jazz. The café is half full, but the crowd's impatience with the slow numbers is waxing. Some rowdier number must come soon or else. Has it become clear yet, they wonder, that there is no answer?

Just a sailboat in the moonlight and you "So," Hannah says, "is there an answer?" Raymond is mute. "I'll take your silence for a no." But he says nothing, neither yes nor no. "What is this, the silent treatment for the suddenly racist Jew? It's not racism, Raymond. It's the fucking situation. You want us to deal with the situation, okay. I'm thinking of my future, and I want Jewish fucking babies, a husband who understands Torah and, say, the Holocaust. It's my life, and you want to paint me like I'm some fucking settler."

182

Raymond meekly intrudes on the silence, to stun his pain a little. "I just wasn't aware that was the situation."

"It is the situation. You want to know what it is and I've told you."

After another minute, he says, "I need to sleep."

That was nothing, I refuse it, and she will regret it, as I regret Lara, and time will give us another breath, and another.

Raymond, afterwards

It is one-thirty, no, quarter to two, when they see the hostel again. After separate showers, Hannah lights Friday night candles, carefully fixing them to the only inflammable surface, which happens to be the toilet top. It is better to light candles than to curse the darkness.

Candles

"Better to light candles than to curse the darkness." Who said it? Bible? Christian? New Testament? Confucius? What I cannot set aside, I cannot set aside, like a prayer over candles that are better than darkness. I will not set aside. Now the barucha. Then again, there's always Jenn and Niklas, still together.

Hannah, afterwards

The clock says 4:15. Rough knocks and the smell of burning plastic. Smoke is pouring out of the bathroom, and Raymond rushes for it while Hannah quickly dresses and sprints to the door to placate the angry, obese man screaming terse

Things are burning

Hebrew. The toilet top has managed to catch fire. Raymond extinguishes the flames by smothering them with a wet towel. "It's out," Raymond shouts. Hannah translates apologetically.

She slowly walks to the bathroom door. There are two identical holes burned through to the water in the tank of the apparently plastic toilet. They should talk, but they return to bed and are both asleep in a minute. It's 4:18.

Returning arrangements

It's 10:22. "I had the strangest dream . . ." Raymond says.

Hannah laughs despite the grossness of the room, the grubbiness of their skin, the smell of burnt plastic lingering in the air. "I wish it had been a dream. Thank Hashem we're leaving." The hostel room is covered in grey flakes the size of postage stamps. Now they have to come to an arrangement. Hannah will pack, straighten, and rush out the front door. Raymond will handle the confrontation.

"You are very very lucky, my friend," says the perky young man at the desk. "Avram stopped fire alarm at last minute. No six hundred shekels."

"We are very sorry."

Avram's friend taps figures into a calculator. "Two hundred for the toilet and seventy-five for room."

Raymond searches for bills of the right denomination.

"May I ask you why?" the man behind the desk asks bluntly. "Why candles on the toilet? Why religion on the place that you shit?"

Raymond shrugs. "I don't know. I'm not Jewish. She is."

The bus drives directly through the Negev, past kibbutzim with their prides of date trees and palms. The highway takes them down from the Red Sea, in a deepening of the earth, to the lowest point on the planet, a desert sea, a dead sea. There the bus stops, and everyone files off for cigarettes and ice cream. Japanese and Indian health freaks bob on the sea's salt surface. From there, everything goes up, through the Judean hills, to Jerusalem, and once again they are lost, in the white heart of the city, flummoxed by silence.

Up and down

There's nothing more to see here. There's nothing more to be here. It's exhausting how the night comes and then day. After fifteen more, I'll be sitting in Toronto with a little history, and no definite plans. What's my idea? What is Raymond doing here? But that's always been the question when he's near. Then I go away. Then he follows.

Hannah considers the rest of May

Bethlehem, obviously. Tomorrow. Wonder if I can walk down somehow. What is the fastest way to pass a security checkpoint? I'll ask Hannah, she'll know. More Old City then. Church of Saint Anne. Something else. Oh, I don't know any more. I guess I'll just keep going to the Dome. Tourists. From the very beginning, and throughout our lives, we are instructed that there is good and bad, right and wrong. Come to a city like Jerusalem,

Raymond considers himself as a tourist

and take sides. Choose your side, and stick to it, and waver.

Hannah considers what affairs mean

Raymond's impure, that's for sure, that's for sure.

Conversation in the night

"What are we doing?" Raymond asks.

Her forearms are resting on him, her fingers playing with the edges of his chest. "What are we doing?" she asks.

"Haven't the foggiest."

"No."

"I have nothing."

"That, I think, is what we have."

She closes her eyes and lays her head down, to rise and fall with Raymond's breath.

What you do when you don't know what to do in Jerusalem

You go to the Wall.

Raymond and Hannah at the Wall

A bar mitzvah is in progress when they arrive. Burly men carry the Torah scroll in their strong arms, and the child seems driven by the ululating voices of the wigged women throwing candy from the partition. Hannah watches from the back end of the square, headscarved by the smoke of her before-prayer cigarette. Raymond watches her, vaguely sick that she is a part of it, then stunned when she goes down to pray.

Raymond considers a pointed theological question

I solemnly avow that religion is bunkum, everywhere it is found and in every form in which it is found. Furthermore, I declare that the acceptance of poorly transcribed, poorly edited manuscripts from prehistoric tribes as the word of the universe itself is a folly that should strain the gullibility of a six-year-old child. I heretofore state without equivocation that religion makes stupidity the way apple trees make apples.

God, I am not a good Jew.

Hannah at the Wall

I'm embarrassed that I don't follow the Law, smoking on Shabbat and all, but worse, I'm embarrassed, for Your sake, at all the silly things You want me to do. Why do You want me to give up bacon forever? What do You care if I light a match on Saturday afternoon?

But here's what I wanted to say: keep my mother and father. Keep danger from the ones I love. Keep Raymond as well. Also, while we're at it, I'm not sure I want life after death if I can't talk in it, like I'm talking now, to the ones I love.

Now a kiss on the stone. And now I go.

There's a Jew who goes down to the Wall to pray every day for twenty-five years. On his way there, he passes an Arab storekeeper. Finally, one day the storekeeper stops him. "Excuse me, but I've seen you go down to the Wall every day for twenty-five years. What are you praying for with such dedication?"

Hannah remembers an old joke

The religious man says, "I go down to the Wall every day, and I pray to God for peace between the Israelis and the Palestinians, and for a lasting peace in Jerusalem."

"And how is it going?"

"Sometimes I feel like I'm talking to a wall."

Naked conversation Hannah rolls off him, and straightens her hair. "We need to get out of Jerusalem."

"How about Bethlehem?"

"Not far enough."

"Back to Elat?"

"How about Hebron?"

Raymond frowns, shakes his head, whistles. "A war zone." Later, they will forget the glib reasonings that brought them to the West Bank, and the fact that they were naked when they decided.

A day in Hebron It's a perfectly beautiful May morning. Hannah packs a disposable camera, a guidebook and money. They will need strength and, so, before their trip, they breakfast at the American Colony Hotel on Nablus Road in East Jerusalem. At the neighbouring tables, blond Midwestern journalists eat cereal with new-found Arab lovers. Ed Bradley, from *60 Minutes,* waltzes through with his coffee. Raymond and Hannah have never tasted food this good together: fruit preserves of luscious texture, perfect poached eggs on toast, bacon for Raymond, pickled mackerel for Hannah, every morsel the freshest. Hannah asks a man carrying a camera sack and a tripod to take a photograph of them with their tiny cardboard contraption. They wash down the flavours with a round of freshly squeezed orange juice, and as they pay (a lot), the waiter brings two large packed lunches to the table (for free). To the waiter, Raymond and Hannah look like poor students who will need refreshment wherever they are going.

In the shared cab, which is the only way into the West Bank, Hannah sits in the back with the women, Raymond up front with the men. At the checkpoint, the whole group must show their papers to a young, embittered soldier who insists on checking the weight of every loaf of bread in an old man's sack. Fifty minutes later they are permitted entry. Raymond desperately wants to turn to Hannah, point out the crooks in the hands of the shepherds in the hills, and say, "Look, they live like David did." And Hannah wants him to know about the woman praying with beads beside her. But the van is silent until they arrive in Hebron.

The first thing they notice is the women, draped and shapeless, formless and sometimes faceless. Hannah, who has worn her loosest shirt and plainest khaki pants, is as exposed as a stripper by comparison. The market has no signs in Hebrew or in English, only in Arabic. They are the only tourists there that day. And if anyone in the market knew Hannah was a Jew, they'd likely try to kill her. Raymond takes out his *Let's Go: Israel*, and holds it to his chest, trying as hard as possible to make them look like what they are, irresponsible Canadian tourists. A camel's carcass adorned with oak leaves hangs in a butcher's stall. In a barbershop, an ad for pantyhose pornographically displays a woman's calf. The towers of the Jewish settlement come into view, and above them, a sign, in English, saying, "This market was built on Jewish land stolen after the 1929 massacre." Raymond brandishes the *Let's Go* like a Bible. They are absolutely lost. They decide to have falafel, two at a shekel apiece.

Despite the eyes of a hundred workless workmen on them, and the laughing children, violent and poor, on their hems, it is the best falafel in the world, better than anything in Jerusalem, New York or Paris. Very simple fresh bread, stewed eggplant, and pickled purple cauliflower. They wonder if they should hide their pleasure, so intense is it.

"What are you doing here?" a stranger in a linen suit and Italian leather shoes asks in Oxbridge English.

Raymond says, "We're here to see the Cave of Macpalah."

All the neighbouring lunchers turn to look. "Please allow me to take you. You will never find it."

"Well, thank you. We're very grateful." They follow him out of the market.

"I'm afraid I can only take you to the Arab side, however. Afterwards, you may try the Jewish side if you wish. Then leave immediately."

"Right."

"Otherwise . . ." He makes a gesture of throwing a stone.

The man leaves them at the gates of the mosque, and they leave him with a storm of thanks.

Six guides flock to show them the place where Baruch Goldstein massacred twenty-nine praying

Muslims. They point through bars at the graves of Abraham and Sarah, Isaac and Rebecca, Jacob and Leah. On the other side, behind another set of bars, Jews are praying. The guides, in exchanges of eloquence, discourse on how three hundred fanatics keep a whole city in terror. After proffering the necessary tips, Raymond and Hannah go to the other side, where quiet men pray into their books, and there are no guides. Instead, a shrine to Baruch Goldstein. Soldiers, bitter and ridiculous, wait outside. The soldiers of the IDF, who look like demigods on the Tel Aviv beaches, like they could lay any girl, like they could hunt down any enemy of the state, are befuddled, defending zealots in some hopeless shit town.

Enough.

In a few whispers, they establish the need to leave quickly. The only way is a shared cab, in which they are again separated, unable to speak to each other. Hannah wants to tell him that they forgot to take pictures. The checkpoint requires an unbearable hour and twenty minutes before they are once again in a country where eyes meet theirs without envy, fear and hatred, and God does not, in every case, equal death. But there's no relief for Raymond and Hannah as they cruise to Jerusalem, to the apartment; no relief of their disgust and self-disgust, anger and contempt. Discussion would be useless.

The moment they're in her room again, Hannah states it directly: "Fuck me."

"I can't," he says, "I just . . ."

She strips naked. "I need something." She lies down, spread out on the bed. Raymond kneels, and licks the threads of her cunt until each muscle in her squeezes shut and opens and she screams the name of God out.

Raymond lies down beside her. A gecko is climbing across the ceiling. Hannah curls into his shoulder and weeps. When he gets up again, he will find two perfectly good uneaten lunches in the backpack, and bring them to the bed.

Goodbyes They wander in and out of a simple problem they cannot solve, like a children's puzzle in a yellowing magazine. Trust. Love. Jew. The words are laid like mines, at odd angles for deliberately random detonation. It ends when Raymond utters, "All right then, you're right," takes his suitcase out of the closet, and slowly shuffles through the armoire for the things that are his. From the desk, he takes his papers, his one book, and from the jars his pens. Hannah is wiped out, staring at the unfolding drama from the bed. He gets to the zipper of the suitcase.

"Wait," she says, "just wait."

Seven days Only a week left. Toronto. But if there have ever been bodies prepared for time to run out, Raymond and Hannah inhabit them. They are as familiar with impending departure as mountain-dwellers are with thin air.

In a week, I'll be back in Toronto, in the spinster university, yes, but in bed with Hannah? Interesting. Yes, I find that particular point particularly intriguing. How will that work, then?

Raymond thinks about time passing

Using the room like a motel now, but no driving away, and no cleaning lady, and the dust doubles and we don't even leave except for food. Toronto. Consider it. Look around for a job, I suppose, and a synagogue. And some nice Jewish guy. Raymond stops it all; better to be up in the air with him than nothing on the ground. Fucking on this narrow, unfortunate twin. Like the first week. Repetition. we make love in places we're about to abandon.

Hannah on the apartment

"What's going to happen with us in Toronto?" Hannah asks.

Conversation over pita, hummus, tabbouleh and fried tomato

"You're the Talmudist," Raymond says.

"What's that supposed to mean?"

"It means you're the one with the mind for impossibilities. I'm done. I'm out."

"Talmud is about endless debate," Hannah says. She shoves three fingers of pita and hummus in her mouth. "We came together. We should be apart, that much I know. There's no reason we're still in the same bed except expense and convenience."

"Listen, I offered to go. If two weeks in a hostel is all it takes, I'll go."

"But you're not going to go. If you were going to go, you'd be gone."

"You're right, it's very good," Raymond says.

"I told you we needed two plates."

"At least."

"Better let it sit." She takes a quick sliver of the burning-hot eggplant. "Nothing is going to be decided here, I'm thinking. Nothing is ever decided in Jerusalem. It's not a place where decisions get made. We had to leave to talk. So maybe we should just wait."

"Wait until Toronto."

"Jerusalem is just too . . . Everything costs too much." She cuts a bit of the skin off to cool separately. "We have to wait. It's not a plan, it's a fact. We're not going to figure it out this month."

"Timing," Raymond offers.

"Call it what you want. Location."

Raymond considers this. "I think it's very smart. And I think this is cool enough."

They chew little pieces, blowing on them and then rolling them around in their mouths. Raymond was wrong. It's still too hot.

"I think this is the best eggplant I've ever eaten."

"Don't say Jews can't cook," Hannah says.

"I never did."

"You can't make this at home. You need the oil to be so hot that it hardens the outside. Then you soak it in lemon."

"It's like steak," Raymond says.

"Do you think it's doable, this vow of silence?" Raymond asks her.

"I think it's tryable."

"Just let it wave over us?"

"Defer," Hannah says. "We have just six days left. Again. We keep doing this. Impossible situations. What are we going to do? I have just six days left in Jerusalem. I can't believe what I'm saying."

Raymond ignores this burst of exasperated desperation. "Wait until we're in a boring city."

"Yes. Wait until we can talk. There's nothing else to do in Toronto. Here, getting out breath takes effort."

Raymond questions this with a pout of his bottom lip, then shrugs. He reaches over to touch her face, and she leans across the table for a reciprocating kiss.

"I have no better ideas. Let me pay the bill."

Though Raymond has walked through the Church of the Holy Sepulchre several times, he has never entered the sepulchre itself; the queue has always been off-puttingly long. The Coptic side, where the Saviour's head supposedly rested, is always available, but what does the head matter? The body is everything. The cupola above shows sunlight, with pigeons. Then there is a tiny antechamber in the edicule, in which the pilgrims must stoop to stand in candle-lit darkness. He waits forty-five minutes to enter the sepulchre proper.

It is a slab. He waited half a movie for a slab. A flat piece of stone. Raymond kneels beside an Armenian nun who is saying perfunctory prayers. It's a low room with a slab. His being there is an absurdity.

Raymond in the
Holy Sepulchre

But he remains kneeling and watches the candles. Hannah. The way her body curls into his at night. Flashes of her screwing him on a chair. The shape of her right leg. The sweetness of her spaced, crooked teeth. Her narrowing, cunning eyes. Clever and dark. It's worth believing in whichever God, Raymond thinks. If religion makes no difference, why not subscribe?

Commentary on Ruth 1:16

"Intreat me not to leave you, or to return from following after you: for where you go, I will go, and where you lodge, I will lodge: your people shall be my people; and your God my God."

Hannah, I would let them cut the tip of my prick off if you would hold it in your hand and on your tongue forever. I will submit my sons to the most ancient cosmetic surgery, and give them baggage to carry the rest of their lives. Let us have five rabbis for sons. I will build a fence around the Law: shellfish will be an indulgence at friends' houses only. When I order pork in a restaurant, there will be a tinge of guilt in each sweet, swinish bite. I will go farther than that: when I eat a cheeseburger, deep in my heart I will feel it a sacrilege. See how the prayer shawl covers my blond hair. Look, the blue border brings out the colour of my eyes. Dancing to crappy Israeli pop, I will shout out, "Blessed are your tents, O Israel!"

How can I, student of Burton, not cherish a religion of difficult, ornately designed texts, or not love the tents of a tribe that has wagered everything,

everything there is, on written-down words? I will plunge into the Torah daily, as I plunge into your flesh.

Hannah is lying on her bed, not reading, not thinking, not speaking, not planning, not sleeping, just being in Jerusalem. Five days left.

Where Hannah is

Never once have I had a dream about Jerusalem that I recall. Not one. Perhaps never a dream about Israel.

Hannah hates Jerusalem

Think, Hannah.

Not here. In the middle of a white city, crowned with a gold dome, crammed with hatred and fear, overflowing with love, I have no dreams. Fuck Jerusalem. Bodies lying on the street.

I dream about Toronto. Moodless city at the margins of the earth. City for the fish that slipped through the parts of the net that are broken. In that open grid, those open neighbourhoods, there's nothing that can't be resolved. Fuck, there's nothing to resolve. But that's what I dream of.

There are only four days until Hannah leaves. The impact of Hellenism on Israelite architecture? Perhaps the way you wipe sweat from your forehead or some grandiloquent turn of phrase will resolve the future tonight. The declaration of statehood? The status of the final status? Who gives a shit when you're in love with a messed-up Jew? When you can recall with utter immediacy an affair with a nineteen-year-old Chinese violinist,

Who gives a shit about Jerusalem?

and are sleeping with the woman you cheated on? Raymond does what he would do in any city. He goes for coffee, only here he's looking up at the Dome, and the gold light reflects the sun back up at it. He also visits the English-language bookstore, which receives the thought-weight dumped from the luggage of each tourist wave. Burton is not among it.

Hannah thinks about another end

What do I do? Depends. Up in the air. Deborah's gone and where are my friends? I won't ask the Jewish girls in the apartment whose minds are like mousetraps. And Jenn: I know what she'll say. Wait and see. Want someone I can trust who will tell me something I don't expect. Who is that? Raymond. He's the talking, kind one. Fuck. What will I do in Toronto the day after I've left, when he's still in Jerusalem?

Why not prepare?

Though he will leave three days after her, Raymond figures he may as well pack while he has company. Hannah finds that the space of the things she has lost or left behind coincides exactly with the space of the things she has acquired. Jerusalem has removed old dresses and old books, and put back six shining, well-used Hebrew texts and more modest clothes.

At the end of the day, they are in a bare room, empty of everything but the bed, the suitcases and themselves. They have just enough time to go out for one last walk.

There's nothing left to say. They look over the Conversation on the walls of the Old City roofs of the Arab quarter, which are bristling with TV antennae and satellite dishes, and to Raymond it's still incredible that people have houses in the Old City, that people cook dinner for their families and screw and shit into toilets in the Old City of Jerusalem. Hannah knows better.

"This is our last last night," Raymond says.

Migrants drift from empty room to empty room Last nights and one last night to another, filling up the world and emptying it, like weather. Raymond and Hannah have known only travel and they could go to the airport tomorrow and find a path through the sky to Beijing, Delhi, Paris, Rio de Janeiro, but their bed has flesh borders. They run up against them to be thrown back, and their calls into the air are laments.

Sweet sixteen, so young-skinned it didn't matter Hannah's lament what I touched, tingle-flesh, pulse-flexed, just so that someone's rough hands were fumbling along me, in my long hair, on the green ground. Yes. A phase only. Now all my learning comes from embarrassing myself. Remember? Slightly only.

Now Raymond. Not tomorrow. I was happy, and he held up a fish in the bedroom, showing me his pride wriggling on a hook at the end of a line, a twelve-year-old boy in his heart. Our bodies decided. Then he wrecked it.

I walked into yeshiva, and my learning was rich, gorgeous, infinite. Then it mattered he's not Jewish.

There is a wall that crumbles just so, I think. The long sighs in the cool bed come to an end. They must. Think about it: cities are constantly raised in height by the dust that covers them. Walls, stone by stone, whimper to emptiness. There is always a packet of remnants under the dirt, some record for the archaeologists. Walls keep being built, keep crumbling, keep remaining. Eventually the whole world will be remnants.

When the sun rises, there will be a day that reaches out, only one. The sky will hold them. They will be an ocean apart. Engines will carry them, sustain them.

Morning comes, the time for leaving. Hannah waits at the corner for the cab, and Raymond follows her down to help with the suitcases.

"There'd be no point in you coming anyway. They wouldn't let you in," Hannah says.

"I'm looking forward to seeing the airport again. I remember it like yesterday."

"You were there yesterday, practically. Don't come."

"I remember it being Israel cubed. The soldiers everywhere. The sense of threat. All that. Here's your cab."

The van pulls up, and Raymond lifts her luggage into the back. Hannah is the last customer of the trip. Two Orthodox families are screaming at each other, the driver, their kids, and maybe the car. The driver begins shouting at Raymond in Hebrew to hurry up. Hannah can only manage a quick wave before the doors slam shut and the cab veers off. No chance for a goodbye, but he does see her mouth the words "See you in Toronto" as he waves back.

Hannah is back in Canada once she steps on the plane: when the stewards announce that cell-phones must be turned off on this non-smoking flight, home is the sound of English and French, one after the other. She is reminded of her child-hood through bilingualism: airports, French class and the cereal box. There will be a dull back-ground roar while she moves 9,342 kilometres to her apartment in Toronto and the future.

Engines

If it be Your will, God, our God, God of the fore-fathers, lead us to peace, and I mean put our feet in the place to guide us, and return us to our homes. Spare us from the hand of the enemy, the ambushes of thieves and animals, and from all the punishments of the earth. Bless our work, and give us grace and mercy, in Your eyes and, if pos-sible, in everyone else's. God who hears prayer hear our prayer as You are God who hears prayer.

Wayfarer's Prayer

There is not even a broom to sweep up the scraps of garbage in the corner. When Raymond turns on the radio, it is to see whether a plane carrying someone he loves has crashed or blown up. When he turns off the radio, he can hear that there are no rivers.

Jerusalem is a bare room

The sun is where it is. Nothing can change that. "Please stay seated until the seat-belt sign has been extinguished," but Hannah wants to stay seated. When she stands up, there will be Toronto. It is a nice day in Toronto. A nice sun shines on a nice yellow field and the nice airport hangar.

On the cab ride through downtown, the skyline holds no attraction for her. The CN Tower is an idiot's bauble, but on the radio the news is bland and the fact cheers her.

She carries her own bags up to the apartment to find that the subletter is gone; the place is just as she left it. Once again, she's alone in an emptiness with two suitcases and a bed. What was that?

Toronto has nothing but space and money. Space and money are something.

I will go to Hannah's body and my books. All my books. The library. I miss it, and I miss Hannah's body. What is the etiquette for whatever situation this is? After a one-week stand, eight-month separation, infidelity, hemi-demi-semi-reconciliation, how long is appropriate before calling? Do I just walk off the airplane and straight to her door? Or do I wait three days before I call, say in the afternoon, faux casually.

In my library, there is a silver Jerusalem you can hold in your hand. There are mint books and ruined. A marble statue that jellies to woman's flesh under the force of a prayer. Sixteen saxophones breathe faintly onto the street in my library. Men like Samson break out of multi-coloured construction paper chains.

I'd gladly burn it down for an hour of cheap sushi with her.

The only city that matters is the one of taxicabs and airports and airplanes, where your location is just a name and your identity is a booklet containing your photograph and a number, and a stamp on the pages for each of your journeys.

City of leaving

Godforsaken Toronto. God will never forsake Jerusalem. God, please never turn Your eyes to Toronto. It's a terrible place to visit. Raymond must be leaving now. God, turn Your eyes away from him. His body as beautiful as a city not cared for much. Forgetting that white city, he comes back to his books, to his library, from one bare apartment to another. His body passes through security, and the airport architecture, to the engine that will bring him to me.

Hannah, in Toronto, considers Jerusalem

A snag. The security guards find Raymond's story suspicious and they take him to an extremely private room for three hours to discuss it. He answers their questions. Yes, he came to visit a woman who was studying at a yeshiva. Yes, she was female and studying Torah. It was Orthodox, yes, but egalitarian. Yes, that is rare. No, she was not exactly a girlfriend, but ... Okay, she was. Is she still? That question is up in the air. She is Jewish, yes. No, he is not. Yes, she went to yeshiva. He did pack his bags himself.

To Toronto

After twenty minutes, he realizes that the security men are right. The story has too many angles. It is implausible. It is nothing but angles. Still, he tells it to them over and over while they rifle through his things, and pierce the fibres of his suitcase with a long needle. The question spins like a wheel.

Finally, Raymond is deemed not a threat. He's the last person to sit down on the plane.

The end Up in the air. The question keeps spinning, yes and no, Jerusalem and Toronto, Raymond and Hannah. Yes or no. On the ground, their bodies will decide.

Their bodies were as beautiful as a city not cared for much. His belly and hers were two bridges facing each other across a ravine. Their hair waved like the flags over the embassies. Their mouths were two open doors leading into a single building and, lying beside each other, they spread out like one smog cloud over two smokestacks. They ran like water, like the subway, from one end of the city to the other.

In Toronto, nothing stays for long. There is space enough here to fit us all in. No one remembers. A city for the fish who slipped through the parts of the net that are broken. The most anyone says in Toronto is, "Look, here were Native, then English, then Jewish, Italian, Portuguese, Vietnamese, and other nations will take their place in a few generations." The most anyone says is, "Look at the Muslims praying in the rush of Kennedy subway station." "Look, we will lose even the idea of mother tongue or nation." There is a dream of interpenetration, and a dream of a city that war never visits.

We are doves, or will become doves, is all the Diaspora dreams allow. Jerusalem has doves. Pigeons are Canadian doves. We are pigeons, multicoloured, rustling against each other in all the public places, and the twenty-first century belongs to the colour smudge.

She left and he stayed. Jerusalem and Toronto. Every other city is built beside the sound of running water, but Jerusalem is built on the sound of water being drawn from deep wells. Jerusalem means "city of peace." No rivers disturb or wash it. She pressed herself against the Western Wall, toward that spot where revelation comes of itself, almost accidentally. She murmured her desires in the cool chalk of the well of souls, in the deep wells that are the laughter at the centre of the earth. She was alone with Jerusalem.

In Toronto, everything had its place by accident on his body. He waited for her in a city of parking lots and exile and imaginary Jerusalems that spring from so many destroyed ones. Then, like a pigeon, he flew into Jerusalem, and in Jerusalem their bodies shifted dust from one place to another. In the unbroken net of her hands, she brought him into the white city. She took his body into her hands as if it were money. She walked into him as if he were an empty room.

The notch in her back was the groove where the cross once stood: he knelt to run his fingers across it. But her breasts were like the stones in the hands of little boys. Her brain was filled with ricocheting bullets, and stray sacks of bombs were picked up by thieves on her beaches. Everything on her body had its place, but be careful where you step. Even unhardened concrete is an appropriate place for memorial candles. Jerusalem is an eye. A thousand years is the blink of an eye. Every stone is precious and everyone remembers why.

She returned to Toronto, and he followed, and followed her body through the moodless city. Through its ragged edges, the suburban sprawl, through the neighbourhoods, the scruff of ravines, the centres of industry, she came to him through the roar of the twined highways and the shadows of the expressway. He felt the world's six billion. It was too much to hope to stumble on her in the crowds.

Somewhere in Toronto is a lake. That's where she found him. Every part requires every part in a city, in a body. His hand on her thigh means her hand on his neck just so. The highway through the ravine means the building of the supermarkets in the suburbs. From her mouth, the smell of magnolias and gasoline and fishrot, and in his eyes, immigrants constantly greeting their families in airports. They were like the waves of the lake touching the rocks beside the expensive condominiums on the shoreline. Children take ferries from it to go to the amusement park.

Again in Toronto, their bodies make the sound of rivers. They taste salt, emerging out of their own rivers. They have become the lake at the end of the city, perfect and serene and calm, and they start up like two pigeons among a flock of sleeping doves in the public grounds of the city. Their bodies are perfect.

Martha Kanya-Forstner. Ann Patty. Maya Mavjee. **Acknowledgements**
Jackie Kaiser. Scott Richardson. Susan Broadhurst.
Gary Stephen Ross. The Canada Council for the Arts.

Temple Israel
Minneapolis, Minnesota

IN MEMORY OF
HARRIET SHADUR
FROM
PHYLLIS GOLDHIRSCH
&
BERTHA ROVELSKY